the Source of Health

Sirshree

The Source of Health

By Sirshree Tejparkhi

Copyright © Tejgyan Global Foundation
All Rights Reserved 2016

Tejgyan Global Foundation is a charitable organization with its headquarters in Pune, India.

Published by WOW Publishings Pvt. Ltd., India

Typeset by InoSoft Systems, Noida

First edition published in 2016

Third Reprint in June 2018

Copyrights are reserved with Tejgyan Global Foundation and publishing rights are vested exclusively with WOW Publishings Pvt. Ltd. This book is sold subject to the condition that it shall not by way of trade or otherwise, be lent, resold, hired out, or otherwise circulated without the publisher's prior written consent in any form of binding or cover other than that in which it is published and without a similar condition including this condition being imposed on the subsequent purchaser and without limiting the rights under copyright reserved above, no part of this publication may be reproduced, stored in or introduced into a retrieval system, or transmitted, in any form, or by any means, electronic, mechanical, photocopying, recording or otherwise, without the prior written permission of both the copyright owner and the above-mentioned publisher of this book. Any person who does any unauthorized act in relation to this publication may be liable to criminal prosecution and civil claims for damages.

*To all those healers,
whose pure presence bestows
true healing and complete health
to countless lives on Earth.*

Disclaimer

The content of this book does not advocate the use of any particular healthcare protocol, but is intended to make information about the effects of thoughts and emotions on health available to the public.

This book has been published to enlighten readers of the health-benefits of consciousness-centric and thought-centric approaches to healing. It is based on the premise that disease is first created at the mental plane through our thoughts before its onset at the physical plane. Therefore, it is paramount to reach the root cause of disease at the subtler plane of our existence.

However, this does not imply that readers should solely rely on the approaches explained in this book. The information contained in this book is not intended as a substitute for consulting your physician or healthcare provider.

Any attempt to diagnose and treat an illness should be done under the direction of a certified physician or healthcare professional. The reader is advised to do so and follow their recommendations in addition to the approaches provided in this book.

The author and publisher hereby disclaim any liability to any party for any loss, damage, disruption, adverse effects or consequences resulting from the sole use of approaches discussed in this book.

Contents

Preface ix

Part I – The Essence of Health

1. Complete Health — 3
2. Understanding the Source of Health — 8
3. Healing from the Source — 17
4. The Remedy For Incurable Disease — 28
5. Healing with the A-Body — 39
6. Understanding and Dealing With Emotions — 52

Part II – The Law of Health

7. The First Law of Health — 67
8. The Second Law of Health — 77
9. The Third Law of Health — 81

10.	The Fourth Law of Health	92
11.	The Fifth Law of Health	103
12.	The Sixth Law of Health	111
13.	The Seventh Law of Health	117

Part III – The Tool for Health

14.	The First Tool – FOCUSED SELF-TALK	131
15.	The Second Tool – GUIDED IMAGINATION	140
16.	The Third Tool – FAITH FAIR BOOK	152
17.	The Fourth Tool – FORGIVENESS	162
18.	The Fifth Tool – GRATITUDE	170
19.	The Sixth Tool – ACCEPTANCE	183
20.	The Seventh Tool – RELEASING	190

Preface

An old man was teaching his grandson about life...

He said to the boy, "A fight is going on within me. It is a terrible fight between two wolves."

The boy looked puzzled, "Who are these wolves that fight within you?"

"One of them is anger, hatred, sorrow, greed, guilt, self-doubt, and ego."

"The other is love, joy, peace, hope, humility, kindness, and faith."

He continued, "This same fight is going on within you too, and also within every other person."

The boy was lost in thought. Finally he asked, "Which wolf will win?"

The old man replied, "The one you feed!"

What are the forces that are playing within us? Which forces are we feeding? Are we nurturing complete health? Are we moving towards higher levels of wellness? Or are we unknowingly feeding disease in various facets of our existence?

The Source of Health provides the key to perfect health discovery. It fills important gaps in our understanding of health and illness. The principles and tools provided in this book can be of help, not only for people dealing with illness, but also for those who want to prevent illness and raise their state of wellbeing.

The Earth is made up of various components. Like air, land, water, plants and animals. For the sustenance of life, it is important to consider all these components as a whole, rather than separating them. This is because what happens to a part impacts the other parts as well.

In the same way, human life, as a whole, is made up of interdependent facets - physical, mental, social, and spiritual. When one facet is not healthy, it causes an impact on all the other facets of life.

Complete health is a state of integrity of all aspects of our existence viz. physical, mental, social, and spiritual. There are five key facets that constitute complete health:

Peaceful mind – A steadfast mind that functions effectively without wavering in testing situations of everyday life.

Fit body – A body that quickly heals itself at the onset of disease. A body that is filled with zest for life. One that is capable of peacefully combating any disease.

Flexible intellect – An intellect that is open to new insights, new ideas and new perspectives, instead of being stubborn and fixed about preconceived notions and past assumptions.

Awakened consciousness – Heightened awareness, wherein the divine light of consciousness dispels ignorance and illumines every aspect of life.

Complete aim of life – A purpose that lends a unified direction to the flow of life through the mind, intellect and body.

The prevailing view about healthcare can be compared to the perspective of an iceberg. Only 10% of the iceberg is visible, while 90% of it is submerged. In the same way, it can be said that all the external visible factors such as medical services, environmental factors, the quality of food, and the increasingly challenging workplace contribute only 10% to our state of wellbeing.

Consider that 90% of the factors that govern our health are actually hidden within us. We can work upon ourselves for this 90% to progress towards complete health.

This does not undermine the other 10%. There is a vast potential for improvement and advancement in medical services, quality of foodstuff, our workplaces and environmental health.

While healthcare is making progress in leaps through scientific breakthroughs, it is more important that we take charge of our own health and change our attitudes towards health.

The key purpose of this book is to empower us to take responsibility for our own health. It enables us to actively participate in our own healthcare, rather than just depending on medical services and therapies to lead us out of illness. It provides practical ways of raising our own health bar, while we continue to work with health practitioners to raise our level of wellness.

Another important purpose of this book is to redirect our focus within ourselves to the foundation principles that govern complete health. It endeavours to address the 90% that is hidden within us, which has the foremost bearing on our health.

Rather than focusing on illness of specific parts of the body, this book focuses on the interplay of the mind and body and the potential health benefits of connecting with the Source– the enlivening consciousness– which is our true nature.

Part I – The Essence of Health sets the foundation for the further parts. It delves into the true meaning of health and wellness. It probes into the nature of who we truly are and how we relate to the mind and body mechanism. It also explains effective ways of healing from deeper levels of our true nature.

Part II – The Laws of Health expounds the seven laws that govern health. These laws determine the interplay between mind and body and show how we can work in alignment with these laws to progress towards perfect health.

Part III – The Tools of Health provides seven effective tools, all of which can be put to effective use *within* us, to transcend illness and raise our level of wellness.

Our mind and body are like a temple of consciousness. When we are unaware of how this temple should be maintained, the darkness of ignorance causes the temple to be subject to impurities. It is now time to bring the light of understanding in this temple. We can then cleanse the temple and restore its resplendence.

The key to perfect health discovery exists within you. Read further to discover this key!

Power of Happy Thoughts

Part I

The Essence of Health

1

Complete Health

What does it mean to be healthy? This question has deceptively deeper implications than what is obvious. The widely prevalent belief is that being healthy means the absence of disease.

If we do not see any obvious symptoms of disease at the physiological plane, we consider ourselves healthy. If our medical diagnostic tests – our blood sugar levels, our haemogram counts, and body scans– hover around the acceptable range, we assume this as a sign of health.

This perspective is not only prevalent among laymen, but also influences the current approach to prevention and treatment of disease. It is a norm to measure health in terms of how often you need to visit a doctor or the results of periodic diagnostic checks. It can be said that Allopathy generally views health in negative terms as the absence of disease and disability, rather than the positive state of health.

While absence of health does result in disease, the absence of disease symptoms need not necessarily mean health.

Health is much more than the mere absence of physical disease and disability. It is a state of complete balance in all planes of life, which include not just physical vitality, but also a stable, balanced and effective mind, harmony in relationships, and most, an alignment with the spiritual purpose of existence.

The World Health Organization has defined health as a complete state of physical, mental and social wellbeing, and not merely the absence of disease or infirmity.

True health lies in the integrity of all facets of our existence – physical, emotional, and social. Supreme levels of health are indicated by the presence of higher levels of joy and peace, reflected as a sense of completeness in oneself, by the unrestricted flow of love, joy and creativity in our lives.

Health and disease are not opposites. They are two states that exist on a continuous scale. At one end of this scale are complete balance, fulfillment and connectedness with our true essence. At the other end are extreme imbalance and disconnectedness from the Source of life, which manifests as physiological dysfunction and emotional disarray, leading to wider expressions of disease, social disharmony, financial struggle and spiritual loss.

Consider that long before diagnosable symptoms appear at the physical level, the seeds of imbalance are sown at a subtler level, which then manifests into body organs and physiological processes. It is much later that physical symptoms of disease begin to appear.

This is true even at a social level. The seeds of disharmony are first sown in the mind much before we begin to sense its manifest form in the dynamics of everyday relationships.

Prevention and treatment of disease – whether physical, emotional, or social – can be complicated and at times ineffective when one tries to primarily address individual symptoms at the superficial level. It can be much simpler and more effective if one also addresses the imbalance at a subtler level within oneself.

In this book, we will address the facet of complete health in the context of the mind-body mechanism.

The results can be phenomenal when we focus on correcting the underlying cause of health problems rather than treating specific symptoms. Multiple symptoms occurring at various levels can have a common underlying cause. For example, stress, indigestion, and ulcers can be dealt with when the common underlying cause is removed by restoring balance at the mental level, while also correcting food habits.

Healing intelligence exists within you

The human immune system comprises of trillions of white blood cells and antibodies designed to locate and destroy specific foreign intruders. Additionally neurotransmitters, genes, and hormones together form a formidable line of defense to counter disease conditions. The body's healing system is a wondrous harmonious orchestra that organizes these lines of defense. The intelligence that functions behind such a marvelous healing system has to exist in wholeness at a higher level, rather than at the level of distinct separate parts.

It is the intelligence within the mind-body mechanism that actually heals; not the medical or healing practitioner.

True healing is not merely about symptom management; rather it is a transformation that occurs from our original nature of wholeness, directed by the in-built intelligence of the mind-body mechanism. At best, doctors can only facilitate and create conducive conditions for this intelligence to effect healing. For example, doctors may prescribe medicine which can help in delaying the spread of bacteria, while the body's healing forces catch up to tackle the disease.

Today, most medical practices in prevention and treatment of disease do not fully believe in awakening the body's self-healing ability. Most disease prevention and treatment efforts are focused primarily on external, technological and pharmaceutical interventions. In many cases, administering powerful drugs can only provide short-term symptomatic relief. In the longer term, they also give rise to side-effects in the physiology, thereby doing more harm than good.

Healing modalities ought to focus on invoking and enhancing this intelligence that is inherent within the mind-body mechanism.

The Source of healing intelligence

The human mind-body is an ever-changing mechanism. It is a finite expression of the underlying wholeness. To understand health and healing, it is of prime importance to understand the source of this wholeness.

What brings the various body constituents together and makes them function so marvelously towards the higher purpose of life? It is obvious that a higher intelligence coordinates the constituents to work in a cooperative manner like the various instruments performing a symphony in an orchestra.

This intelligence controls body temperature by dynamically sensing the atmosphere around it through a system called thermoregulation. It regulates and fine-tunes the secretion of hormones to ensure that the physiology functions at an optimum level. It regenerates and renews worn out or wounded tissue. It mends fractures in bones. Reproduction to ensure continuity is also built into the mind-body mechanism.

What is this invisible essence that organizes and intricately coordinates these parts and aligns them to the purpose of the whole mind-body entity?

It is the nature of our wholeness that expresses as this intelligence through the human mechanism. Hence, at the onset of disease, it can be more effective to focus on restoring the expression of this wholeness, while tending the diseased parts.

It follows that to understand health, we need to first understand the Source of wholeness, the wellspring of intelligence that regulates and heals the mind-body mechanism. We will explore the nature of this Source and the mind-body mechanism in the next chapter.

2

Understanding the Source of Health

Every day, we engage in the world and operate through our thoughts, our feelings, the words that we speak or write, and resultant actions through our body. We operate in the dimension of thoughts, feelings and physical experiences through the body.

The source of thoughts, feelings and physical action exists beyond them. It exists beyond the mental and physical realms. The Source pervades all manifestation. It is the screen of consciousness on which the movie of life is being projected. This screen is the creator, projector, substratum and also the experiencer of the movie of life.

Awareness is the nature of the Source. Pure awareness, or pure wakefulness, brings about the manifestation of forms and phenomena. Our mind, comprising thoughts and feelings, is the expression of pure awareness. Our body is a denser, more obvious expression of the Source, a grosser expression of the subtler mind.

The Mind-Body Mechanism

The human mind and body emerge in that sequence as an expression of the Source. As energy becomes denser, it takes the form of thoughts, feelings, emotions, and intellectual faculties. This constitutes our mental body, which can also be called the A-Body or Auric body or Subtle body. It can be called the A-Body also because it is of A-priority when we consider health and healing. The A-Body is supple, pliable and impressionable. It is invisible to our gross senses of eyesight, hearing, and touch in the physical realm.

The grosser manifestation of energy takes the form of our physical body and its physiological processes, which can be called as the B-body or Biological body or gross body.

The B-body also includes the *Pranic* layer (the vital energy sheath) comprising the *chakras* (energy vortices) and meridians (energy channels). The chakras are whirling vortices of energy that take in universal energy and distribute it through the meridians.

At the physical level, the B-body is composed of five basic elements viz. Space, Air, Water, Fire, and Earth. Space is the subtlest and Earth is the grossest of these elements. The expression of these five elements in various combinations gives rise to physiological components called *Doshas* viz. *Vata*, *Pitta*, and *Kapha*. Vata is formed by the combination of Space and Air. Water and Fire constitute Pitta. Water and Earth combine to create Kapha. The health of the human mind and body hinges on the delicate balance of these *doshas*. Imbalance in the relative proportions of these three components reflects in our mental and physical wellbeing.

All creative processes are enlivened by the sheer presence of pure consciousness, the Source. Creation proceeds from the subtler to the grosser form. The A-body, being the subtler of the two, contains the intelligence that directs the organizing and healing processes of the B-body.

The A-body is invisible to the gross physical senses of the B-body. However, it expresses through the B-body. It is like breeze which is invisible, and yet expresses through the movement of leaves.

This gives rise to the question: Who are we?

You can observe your thoughts. You can also observe your body. This implies that you stand apart from your thoughts as well as your body. Who you truly are is beyond thoughts, beyond the body.

Let us try to understand our true nature to the extent that words can explain.

Consciousness – our true nature

We cannot understand the Source in terms that we would understand any other subject, because it is the Source that enables us to understand everything. Concepts and their explanations belong in the realm of thoughts. Pure consciousness can only be experienced by *being* it.

The human mind-body is an instrument that serves as a medium for the Source to experience itself and express its divine qualities.

It is difficult to capture the true nature of the Source with mere words. For example, when you learn that the experience of the

Source is constantly going on within each of us, you might imagine that this entity exists *within* the human body. Though it may be considered to be logically true, the Source is not just within the body. Consciousness, as we have discussed earlier, pervades the totality of manifest world. Rather, the body is enlivened within consciousness.

Think of a fish living in water. Water is the most obvious and all-pervading presence for the fish. It is the essential medium that enables the fish to be alive. Water exists within the fish and also all around it. Water is so close to its eyes that the fish doesn't realize that it's in water. What if the fish swam off in search of water, asking, "Where is water?"

This is precisely what even the questioning mind would ask when it is told about all-pervading consciousness. "Where is this consciousness? Is it within me, or elsewhere?"

The experience of presence or consciousness is so close to us, in fact, it is our very essence! The Source is present everywhere, within and all around. If we carefully observe, even the locational concepts of *within* and *outside* belong in the realm of thoughts. From the standpoint of the Source, there is neither *within* nor *outside*.

Actually there is no 'we' that exists apart from the Source. There can be no separation – it is only for the purpose of explanation that we separate ourselves from the Source. We are inseparable beingness at the very core. Our living presence is the experience of the Source.

When water occupies a container, it takes on the shape of the container. Though water in essence is formless, when it occupies a cup, it becomes a 'cup of water'; upon occupying a vessel, it becomes a 'vessel of water'. The cups and vessels with their shapes and designs, gain precedence over what they are actually meant to contain.

Like water, the Source, which is the real subject of all experience, assumes the form of whatever it gets associated with. By being associated with the human body, the Source identifies itself as the body. This tendency to identify with individual forms leads to the false perception of diverse separate individuals.

Whatever is inside the skin is 'me' and everything else is 'not me'. We have been living with this illusion without questioning it, because we find everyone else around us living in the same illusion.

This illusion is complete when the flip-side of "I... me... mine" is also imagined into existence – and whatever is 'not me' is shaped into 'you... we... they... it'. This illusion is the root cause of all suffering, struggle, various defilements such as fear, anger, hatred, ill-will, and jealousy and consequent disease.

It is important to be clear about our true identity. Our true nature is consciousness. The mind and body are mere expressions of consciousness. Forgetfulness of who we truly are leads to false identification with who we are not. We identify with our mind and body.

So, this brings us to a major missing link of health: Disease does not happen to us. It happens to the mind-body mechanism.

When you marvel at a painting, you also realize that you have a pair of eyes that help you experience the painting. Similarly, detecting a fragrance or odor lets you know that such a smell exists, but you also realize the existence of your nose. While you listen to music, you also realize the presence of your ears, taste helps you understand the existence of your tongue, and touch provides you with understanding the presence of your skin and nerves.

Viewed in this context, what are thoughts for? The fact that thinking is taking place serves as an indication to the presence of the Source, of consciousness from which all thoughts arise.

When thoughts cease to pull attention, the ever-present stillness behind thoughts is revealed, and consciousness becomes self-aware. The Source becomes aware of itself, leading to the experience of wholeness.

It is not possible for the painting to see your eyes viewing it. Your eyes see the painting and that is proof enough that the eyes exist. In the same way, thoughts can never know the Source. The Source alone can know itself.

Disconnectedness from our true essence

When Consciousness gets identified with the human body, it *becomes* the body. It gives rise to the false notion that 'I am the body'. This is a state of the entanglement that arises from an innate tendency of forgetting one's original nature.

When the awareness of the Source for the its own presence rises, then clarity is experienced. Wholeness and fulfillment are experienced at all levels – physical, mental, social and spiritual.

To the extent that awareness of the Source is focused on itself, it can be said that consciousness is higher to that extent.

When the awareness of the Source is directed towards the diverse world of forms and phenomena, it gives rise to clouding and confusion. The focus of awareness gets limited and invested into dual opposites such as joy and sorrow, pleasure and pain, life and death, love and hatred, light and darkness.

To the extent that awareness of the Source moves away from itself and gets diffused in the duality of the manifest world, it can be said that consciousness is lower to that extent.

The loss of self-awareness leads to attachment to the aspects of the manifest world. Awareness is withdrawn from the Source and gets invested in the details of the world. The wholeness of the Source is shadowed when the mind is absorbed in the objects of perception.

As a result of forgetting our essential nature, we begin to cling onto a false idea about our identity; an idea that is implanted by the belief-systems that we inherit through birth and upbringing of the physical body.

We become disconnected from our essential nature. Wholeness or pure consciousness – which is our true nature – is lost to us. The nature of wholeness gets fragmented and is replaced by a false illusion of separatness and limitation. This is the origin of imbalance.

This fragmentation of wholeness has a ripple effect on wellbeing at all levels of the human mind-body mechanism – both mental and physical. It cascades into the functioning of our physiological processes, causing an imbalance in the physiological components viz. *Vata*, *Kapha* and *Pitta*. It is this imbalance that triggers the proliferation of disease conditions in the body.

Take the example of light reflected from a mirror. A clean mirror surface reflects light completely. However, if the mirror surface is clouded or dusty, it is unable to reflect the full resplendence of light. Similarly, forgetting our true nature leads to clouding and impurities in our perception. The wholeness of who we are is lost in this false perception. The mind-body mechanism is like a mirror that reflects the presence of the Source. False perception causes this reflection to be tainted.

Wholeness is the basis for the intelligence that functions through our human bodies. This gets tainted due to our disconnectedness from the Source. It begins to reflect at the mental level in the form of emotional clutter, defeatist tendencies, intellectual clouding and lack of vitality.

This, in turn, causes impairment in the regulatory tuning of our physiology. With the loss of wholeness, physiological imbalance and lack of coordination set in. This is the seed of disease. Take the example of cancer. Malignancies are caused by cellular misalignment and dysfunction. Cells begin to lose the larger purpose of wholeness to which they belong. This causes them to deviate from their original duplication pattern, leading to rapid proliferation of malignancy.

The primary disease, thus, is the loss of connectedness with our essential nature, a clouding that results from the loss of awareness of who we truly are. Everything else is merely a cascaded effect of this primary disease.

Separation from who we truly are, leads to notions such as: 'I am separate', 'I am superior', 'I am inferior', 'I am dark', 'I am fair', 'I am a Hindu'... Muslim, Christian, I am smart, dull... I am successful, a failure... the list goes on. This is the world of limitations that we imprison ourselves into. This strengthening of a separate limited 'I' is the birth of ego. The ego casts a shadow on the grandeur of our true nature. It restricts the flow of life due to assumed limitations.

Our perception leads to our experience of life. When we look through red glasses, everything appears shaded in red. Our experience of health, relationships, and overall about life is shaded by our perceptions. Our perception is influenced by who we are. If we assume ourselves to be the limited mind-body, then we subject ourselves to the vulnerability of the mind-body. When we realize and abide in our true nature of wholeness, our experience of life at all levels will reflect wholeness.

3

Healing from the Source

Presence is existence; it is consciousness, it is bliss. 'Presence' is one word that points to the experience of the Source.

Presence comes first; thinking comes later. To think, you have to first be. Presence is your true nature. It is the most obvious truth about you.

Yet, presence is lost in the constant chatter of thoughts. Thinking cannot lead to the experience of presence. To experience presence, we need to be aware of what always *is* at any moment.

Descartes, the Greek philosopher, had said, "I think, therefore I am". However, if existence were dependent on thinking, then we would not exist if we were to stop thinking. This is certainly not the case. When we are in deep sleep, we do not think. And yet, we do exist. We even comment on waking that we had sound sleep. We have to exist during deep sleep to be able to know that we did sleep well.

Your presence is independent of thought. Your presence just *is*.

The sense of presence is the simple truth that we are constantly and spontaneously aware of. It is because we are present that we engage in all kinds of activities.

Presence is the most obvious experience. It is the open secret – so open and obvious that we easily fail to notice it. The sense of presence is ongoing ceaselessly ever since our body was born. We may change our identity from being a child to becoming an adolescent, from a youth to a middle-aged family maker, from a student to one who earns a living, from a parent to being a grandparent. However, the sense of presence remains unchanged; it remains constant. If you were to take away all the roles that you consider yourself to be, you would still exist.

The Power of Presence is put into effect when Presence becomes aware of itself, when "I am aware that I am", when consciousness becomes conscious of itself. It is about being present to the living presence, being aware that you exist. It is about being awake to the light that shines upon everything that is being known.

Consciousness creates thoughts as a reflective medium to reflect its light back on itself. When the light of consciousness reflects from the medium of thoughts, back on itself, it is self-illumined. Thoughts – whether they are trivial and mundane, or brilliant and revolutionary – serve merely as a medium to convey the presence of the Source.

To dwell in the experience of the Source, you need to shift your attention from the body-mind to Consciousness. Turn back your attention from the objects of perception to that which enables you to perceive, from thought to that which enables you to think. You will then rise above the changing and limited to that which is changeless, eternal and boundless.

When you abide in awareness of Presence, you go beyond the body. Bodily sensations may continue to be felt, actions may happen, but there will be a constant awareness of this formless Presence, of just being alive. The more you practice being aware of Presence, the more it will become obvious in and through your everyday activities.

The Contrast Mind eclipses Presence

Our mind is originally like clear water, which reflects Presence. However, it becomes impure when impregnated with thoughts of the separate individual 'I'. It is these thoughts that are the grime of ego. The intake of impure water is harmful to health. Just as pure water is vital for the health of the body, similarly it is essential to have a pure mind that reflects our Presence.

All of us have an aspect of mind that can be called the Contrast mind. During infancy, every child remains in the experience of pure presence. However, as the child grows, the parental programming and social conditioning lead to the formation of the contrast mind.

The contrast mind is that facet of the mind that needlessly discriminates, compares and judges everything. The contrast mind is the constant chatter of thoughts that ceaselessly comments about everything that is experienced. It labels objects, beings or experiences as good or bad. It dwells in duality. It draws assumptions about everything. Whenever we notice ourselves thinking, 'This shouldn't have happened... That should have happened...,' it is the contrast mind that is at work.

The contrast mind causes us to be stuck in the vicious cycle of polarities such as joy and sorrow, love and hatred. This aspect of the mind is caught up in imagined notions, presumptions and beliefs. As a result, it triggers fear, worry, angry and depression. It is this facet of the mind that dwells in past memories or the imaginations and anxieties of the future. Due to this, we are lost to the eternal present moment.

These characteristics of the contrast mind do not allow us to accept the present moment as it is. Non-acceptance of the present moment is the root cause of all sorrow and disease. It is due to the harmful nature of the contrast mind that people are forced to consume sleeping pills.

The contrast mind shrouds the sense of Presence. It is like the eclipse that hides the sun of consciousness that is ever-present. It is an unnecessary facet of the mind that causes sorrow and disease. Hence it needs to be transcended to restore true happiness, peace and higher consciousness.

The Power of Formless Presence

To transcend the contrast mind, we need to acquire the art of being in pure formless presence. People who perform their labors in this manner, bring presence to their thoughts, feelings, words and actions.

When we operate from this formless presence by not assuming

ourselves as a mind or body but knowing ourselves as conscious presence, events in our lives will automatically steer their course towards the ultimate goal of life. This is the beauty of formless presence.

The Power of Formless presence allows us to fully witness, to accept, to allow, and be open to whatever we are experiencing, no matter how challenging it may seem to be.

Problems, be it physical disease or otherwise, persist to the extent that we fail to be fully present with them. We tend to resist problems and do not face them with complete acceptance.

Problems cannot be solved by being within the framework of the problem. One has to be outside the problem to be able to clearly see it for what it is. Clearly see it without even labeling it as a 'problem'. Just be present non-judgmentally and allow Presence to take its natural course.

When we can simply be with a situation, without judging or trying to change it, being the experience of pure presence, a space is created around the situation that naturally causes it to move towards the most appropriate solution.

When you bring your conscious presence into those areas of your life, or to those parts of your body that are out of harmony, it gets a chance to allow your in-built healing abilities to function and restore harmony in these areas.

Sometimes, the most powerful approaches are the simplest. The healing power of presence is the deeply transformative. The only way to be convinced about this is to practice it!

Research on the effects of Self-awareness on physical health

As infants, we were in the experience of our true nature. We have abided in the bliss of the Source. However, we have shut ourselves out to the experience of pure consciousness by identifying with the chatter of thoughts.

Scientists have conducted experiments on infant brains and found that infant brains have phenomenal adaptability and learning ability due to the fact that they exist in a thoughtless state most of the time. Electro-Encephalogram (EEG) studies have revealed that brain-waves in infants exist in the theta and alpha range, which means very low mental activity. Pure awareness functions without filters in infants. Hence, infants are free from anxiety, stress and depression. Their bodies heal faster and demonstrate immense resilience.

EEG studies on adults, shows up the constant chatter of the mind as strong beta waves. This constant noise of thoughts is the primary cause of reduced learning abilities when we physically and mentally age. The constant chatter of the mind and deep-set mental conditioning lead to increased probability of stress, anxiety, depression and a general lack of fulfillment, no matter how hard we work to achieve worldly goals.

Meditation practices to access and dwell in the Source lead to reduction in mental clutter, opening up the possibility for universal intelligence to function at its highest potential through our body-minds.

Meditation practices can be broadly classified into two types: Attention meditations and Self-awareness meditations. Attention meditations are exercises of mindfulness where you are focused on what's happening. You are focused on *experiences*.

Self-awareness meditations are exercises where you are aware of the *experiencer*. You use what is being experienced merely as a pretext to be aware of *awareness*.

Research has shown that people who practice Self-awareness meditations exhibit significantly improved quotients of creativity, emotional intelligence, and productivity, besides feelings of happiness, empathy and compassion. The practice of Self-awareness meditations raises the level of awareness of Presence, thereby effecting changes at the emotional and neurological planes.

When you access the Source through the practice of meditation, you are actually loosening the connections of particular neural pathways that enact the programmed fight-or-flight response in the brain. They also strengthen connections of those neural pathways that link to reasoning and higher discrimination.

The field of epigenetics refers to the science that studies how the development, functioning and evolution of biological systems are influenced by forces operating outside the DNA sequence, including environmental and energetic influences.

With evidence growing that raising Self-awareness can have positive health effects, researchers have sought to understand how these practices physically affect the body. A new study by researchers in Wisconsin, Spain, and France reports evidences of specific molecular changes in the body following a period of Self-awareness meditation practice.

The study investigated the effects of a day of practice of Self-awareness mediation in a group, compared to another group of untrained control subjects who engaged in quiet non-meditative activities. After eight hours of practice, the meditators showed a range of genetic and molecular differences, including reduced levels of pro-inflammatory genes, which in turn correlated with faster physical recovery from a stressful situation.

Research by geneticists have also found that in cancer patients, Self-awareness meditation is associated with healthier levels of the stress hormone cortisol and a decrease in compounds that promote inflammation.

Scientific evidence of the Power of Observation

Revelations from research in the field of quantum physics have revolutionized our perspective of the essence of wholeness and the power of observation, popularly called the 'observer effect'.

Physicists performed an experiment of passing electrons through a double-slit. When an electron wave was made to pass through the double-slit and fall upon a photographic film, it created a pattern of striations, indicating wave-interference. This suggested that the electrons were behaving like waves (energy).

However, when scientists tried to *observe* the electron, they found that it *chose* a particular slit, as if it were a particle.

When scientists made attempts to watch electron behaviour, the outcome of experiments was influenced by their assumptions and what they expected to observe!

So, what does that mean for us? It implies that an observer modifies the world merely by observing it! The power of observation is phenomenal. It can cause changes in the material world.

It has also been experimentally proven that detached observation from higher awareness can bring about healing, not just of disease, but of any situation or state of the world!

Healing from the Source through observation

We will now practice healing from the Source through Self-awareness.

Step 1: Connect to the Source

Close your eyes and watch your thoughts as they pass by. Don't judge them. Simply observe them as they continually pass by. Watch as thoughts come and go. Allow this to occur. Let them continue in a normal, natural manner.

Some thoughts may be positive, some negative, some may be related to your work, while others may surface without context. Allow them to pass regardless of the type of thoughts that arise.

Watch the thought, let it pass without chasing it, and silently utter the word "Next." The word "Next" acts as an anchor, allowing thoughts to reach their natural conclusion and dissolve.

Saying "Next" raises your awareness of the gap between the thought that's receding and the next thought that's appearing. This interval may be as momentary as a thousandth of a second, but focus on that point regardless of the length of time.

In that interval there is no thought... everything has stopped and is frozen in that moment. In this gap, you begin to sense the silence in the background of thoughts. In this stillness, you connect with the experience of the Source.

You don't need to be worried if you miss the gap; instead, simply pay attention to the next thought and allow it to pass. The goal of this practice is not a tangible result. The actual purpose is to become aware of the presence of the Source by being in the gap between thoughts.

The key is to just watch these thoughts as if they were clouds passing by, momentarily shrouding the sunlight – clouds that are far away, that don't affect you. Observe these thoughts with a detached feeling, as if you are a witness watching them from afar.

This is one of the most powerful and, surprisingly, easiest ways to connect to the Source. If done properly, it takes just a few minutes.

Step 2: Invoke the Source to begin healing

Bring the organ or disease that needs healing into your awareness. Just notice the organ or disease in a detached manner by resting in the stillness of the Source. This simple noticing, itself, begins healing.

During this step, it is important to continue to be in the stillness of the Source. Let thoughts of the disease or emotions associated with the organ not cloud the experience of the Source. Allow all such thoughts to pass by.

Continue watching the organ or ailment that requires healing from the Source. When you witness in this manner, you are not intending to enforce any particular result. You merely watch with a feeling of detachment and compassionate grace.

Step 3: Stop the healing process based on the feedback feeling

After a few minutes of noticing from the Source, an intuitive feeling will arise from within that healing is underway, whether you notice or not. This feeling comes as a deep assurance that healing is done.

As your feelings change from negative to positive, you experience a deep knowing that positive change has begun.

The third step may be a bit difficult to grasp. If you are used to meditation, then you would be able to sense intuitive feelings.

The most effective and miraculous cures in the world are the simplest. Healing from the Source is so simple that one may tend to distrust the efficacy of this healing modality. The proof of the pudding is in eating it. It is only through practice and direct experience that one can develop faith in it.

For those who are not tuned to meditation or the experience of the Source, healing through the A-Body could prove to be more effective. This is introduced in the next chapter.

4

The Remedy For Incurable Disease

The ultimate medicine is the knowledge of the simplicity and efficacy of the laws of nature. Natures' laws are simple and straightforward. The foremost and most effective treatment for health is simple and straightforward.

When people listen to some complicated names of disease conditions, they begin to think that the condition is grave and that the treatment will be difficult. The most powerful and effective treatment is simple. If one is able to understand and see this during illness, it is easy to regain health. The mind cannot easily accept that the remedy can be so simple, given that it is surrounded by a plethora of information about medical conditions and conflicting views on treatment modalities.

The will to become healthy plays a pivotal role

Simplicity becomes a difficulty so long as people do not get desired results. The mind tends to wonder how the solution to an ailment can be so simple. Consequently, we neglect the most powerful approaches to healing merely because of their simplicity.

Some ascetic healers in Tibet experimented by actually making the simple solution appear to be difficult, so that people would then feel it worth trying the treatment. The healers would ask people to climb up the hills and meet them at the summit. Those who reached the hilltop to receive the treatment were actually raising their will to become healthy. Those who were not even willing to become healthy would not even make effort to reach the hilltop.

Those who were willing were called to the hilltop and imparted the easy treatment. When they climbed up the mountain and learned the simple technique, they were cured because they were willing to apply it due to an increased level of faith in the efficacy of the treatment.

If one had been told of the same treatment at the base he would have long forgotten it. He would have applied it for a few days and seeing no immediate results he would have left it, without persisting with it. Hence, people giving knowledge about health thought of innovative ways to create the will among health seekers to become healthy. Without the will to be healthy, one cannot become healthy. The will to become healthy plays a big role.

When people who do not have symptomatic complaints are asked to do something about their health, their will to exert themselves to raise their health quotient will not be so strong. Their motivation to become healthier will be low. One might feel that he is leading a relatively healthy life without aches or ailments even without exercising his body. Hence, in such cases, the will to move up to the next level of health is not awakened.

But if a sick person's will is strengthened, he longs for health. He immediately starts working on recovering his health. Hence, the adopted techniques ensured that they were simple and raised the will to become healthy. Those who are sick will no doubt work. Even if we are already healthy we should kindle our will to raise our health quotient consistently so as to prepare the mind and body for higher expression of life.

Healing with the A-Body

We tend to give importance to the visible aspects of life. Hence, we deal with life in terms of tangible aspects. Wind or breeze is invisible. Yet, they have the power to drive clouds and cause rain, which sustains life. We see the visible expression of light and sound through our lamps and music players at home, but tend to miss the presence of the invisible electric current that drives them in the unseen.

It is the power of thoughts arising from the Source that directs energy to manifest. We can create the life that we aspire for more effectively when we deal at subtler levels of reality. At the mind-body level, we can bring about transformation in our state of health by invoking the power of the A-Body. Let us understand what this means.

Everyone considers you as a B-Body – the outer, biological mind-body mechanism. Hence, you become habituated to the assumption that you are the B-Body. We are so focused on the physical dimension of life that we do not generally go beyond the physical plane to connect with the subtler dimension of our existence.

When we go deeper, we can connect with the inner mind-body mechanism, the A-Body. This deeper aspect of the mind-body is of A-priority. Since it is intangible, we give it B-priority (secondary importance).

The B-Body is comprised of the gross physical body and the vital energy sheath. The A-Body is our subtler mental body which drives the B-Body. The A-Body is supple and impressionable. It is malleable and can be easily instructed to amend its nature. The A-Body also carries the blueprint of perfect health, in addition to deep impressions from life experiences. It has the ability to recall and reinstate the original healthy state of any physical part or physiological function of our B-Body.

The A-Body first gets the inspiration to become healthy or the tendency to become ill. Later on, the effect gets expressed at the physical plane in the B-Body. Long before a disease manifests in the physical body, its seed is sown in the mental plane in the A-Body. When this deeper truth is missed, one attempts healing only at the plane of the B-Body. But the primary effect always occurs at the plane of the A-Body.

This is as though you are seated in a small box. This small box is then placed into a bigger box. The bigger box is operated through controls that are placed in the smaller box. You are actually handling the small box, but externally it appears as though the bigger box is being handled. It is like riding a motorcycle which has the body of a car attached around it. Visibly, it appears as though you are driving the car, but actually you are operating through the motorcycle.

In the same way, you handle your B-Body through the A-Body. Hence, when there are symptoms of disease at the physical plane, where should you begin the treatment? If you treat at the right point, the results can be miraculous. You should deal and effect changes through the A-Body.

When the A-Body changes, these changes are reproduced in the dimension of the B-Body. When people don't know this secret, they continue to try superficial modes of treatment.

The remedy for incurable diseases

Many people are told that the disease that they are suffering from is chronic and incurable. They believe that they have an incurable disease. They may have tried various therapies and found that the disease still persists.

There is indeed a remedy for such diseases that are deemed incurable. When a disease is said to be incurable, it only means that now the cure for the disease exists within you!

It means that the only remedy is now present within the one who is ailing, nowhere else. External remedies will not help anymore. One now needs to draw out the remedy from within and put it into effect persistently.

Consider this. Suppose that the house in which you live, replaces a brick every day. Unknown to you, each day, an old brick is taken off and replaced by a new one. Further, suppose that even the beams and columns are replaced little by little in a year. The wall paint also changes its shade gradually. It's likely that you will never come to know about this subtle change that is taking place because the house looks the same and changes are so gradual.

If this were to happen, unknown to you, your house would be completely new in a couple of years. The house where you stay today would be completely new with regards to the one in which you were staying few years ago. But you will feel as though its the same old house. It has the same energy, the same vibrations.

Your physical body, your B-body, through which life expresses itself, too is like such a house. You may claim that you are 20… 30 or 40 or more years old. But how old, really, is your B-body?!

What does science say about body re-generation?

There is a general agreement among biologists that the human body regenerates every seven years. Dr. Frisen, a stem-cell biologist at the Karolinska Institute in Stockholm proved that most of the body's tissues are under constant renewal and the average age of all the cells in an adult's body may turn out to be as young as 7 to 10 years. That means you may believe that you are say 45 years old, but your cells are only 7 years young, because they are constantly dividing, regenerating and dying.

Research publications reveal that:

- Lungs are fully renewed every 3 to 4 weeks.
- The intestines renew their inner lining every 3 to 4 days.

- Red blood cells are regenerated every 4 months.
- The epidermis (the outermost layer of the skin) is renewed every two weeks.
- Parts of the liver are completely regenerated every six weeks and the whole liver in 8 to 10 months.
- Bones and the entire human skeleton are replaced every 8 to 10 years in adults.

Till a few years ago, it was believed that the cells of the heart and brain cells are the only parts of the body that do not change. But, even this has now been disproved. It was believed that the heart does not generates new muscle cells after birth. Recent research has conclusively proved that the heart as a whole does generate new cells.

There was a belief that brain cells do not regenerate and that humans are just born with a fixed set of brain cells that complete the circuit during childhood. But in 1988, it was proved that new neurons (brain cells) are born in the brain even in adults. Similarly, the long held belief that the spinal cord cannot repair itself was disproved in 2007 at the Johns Hopkins University in the U.S.

There is growing work, not just on cell regeneration, but complete body organ regeneration too. Scientists like Dr. Alan Russell, Director, McGowan Institute for Regenerative Medicine say that if a starfish can re-grow its fin, if an elk can re-grow its horn, even humans can, since there is evidence other mammals can. Our body has the ability to re-grow organs that are diseased or even severed as evidenced in the human foetus that can re-grow organs in the mother's womb.

Why does disease then linger?

Now the transformative question... If our body is constantly changing and being renewed, why does one still continue to have chronic diseases? Just think about it...

People have caught hold of so-called incurable terminal or chronic diseases. With the renewal of cells, the disease should have ideally vanished from the body. The body that had the disease actually is no longer there. If nothing has remained, then what makes the disease linger?

It is seen that only the belief that the disease is there has caused it to remain. One holds onto the assumption, "I am still the same old body with the disease". When one holds onto the belief of disease and gives it attention, one keeps the disease alive.

Nature is doing its best by changing and renewing the body, but man preserves the disease. How? By indiscriminately focusing on the disease with negative thoughts.

When we constantly repeat certain thoughts, they get reinforced within our subconscious mind as beliefs. Beliefs are like roofs. A roof cannot stand by itself; it needs pillars. The roof of belief needs pillars of evidence. Without the pillars of evidence, the belief will collapse. The more evidences you acquire, the more pillars you're providing for the roof of the belief; the stronger the belief becomes.

Eventually the belief becomes so strong that we are sincerely convinced about the world as we perceive it. We begin to believe our deep-rooted stories, such as: there is always injustice in the world, life is meant to be a painful journey, people cannot be trusted, etc. Given enough time and repetition, a strange thing happens. The roof of belief becomes so strong that it does not require the pillars of evidence any more. It stands on its own. In effect, a belief becomes an undisputed truth for us. These beliefs then perpetuate themselves in our daily lives by manifesting conditions that resonate with them.

An example illustrates this very well. A person attending an evening party encountered a lady who had adorned her hair with flowers. Seeing the lady, he got into a fit of sneezing as he was allergic to this flower. He continued to sneeze and point towards her hair. The lady plucked a flower from her hair and showed him that it was made of plastic. He was at once, miraculously cured!

You know that there was nothing miraculous about this. There was never a disease. The sickness was triggered by his belief that he would suffer the allergic reaction to an actual flower.

So then what is this remedy? We have seen that the physical body is renewed. New cells replace old ones. Any disease that infests our bodies should ideally disappear with the renewal of our bodies. Yet the disease condition continues due to limiting beliefs that are held in the mind. These beliefs perpetuate themselves into new cells in the form of inherited cellular memories, causing the continuance of disease.

When we contemplate upon this in depth, we will be able to zero down on the actual remedy, which is to release our limiting beliefs and inculcate beliefs that are progressive and wholesome. You can achieve this simply by communicating with your A-Body.

The remedy lies in building doubtless conviction in the following fundamental truths about healing:

- Our limiting beliefs cause diseases to persist.
- Beliefs can be changed at a deeper level.
- The A-Body has the ability to restore the natural healthy state of the body.
- The A-Body can be actioned by invoking its abilities and instructing it to do so.

When you build conviction in this understanding, there will be no reason left for diseases to remain. The body in which the disease was present is no longer there. We need to remember this and invoke the abilities of the A-Body for the healthy renewal our body. You will then assert to yourself every day, '*Now I have a new body… The effect of the old disease is no longer present… I am now free from disease.*' You will be able to affirm this to yourself with conviction.

Without the understanding, this assertion wouldn't work as you would lack conviction in this powerful statement. But now that you have understood the truth behind it, you can be established in a firm conviction regarding this. Why can you be free from disease? Because you are merely dropping an assumption. Everything is a game of beliefs; understanding is the whole thing. So whether the disease happened due to external factors such as pollution or improper food intake, or due to internal reasons such as negative emotions, we can apply the understanding and rally the abilities of the A-Body.

You may do everything that it takes in the sense of prevalent therapies. You may take the dosage of medicines recommended by the doctors. But along with it, this understanding will speed up the healing, thereby restoring health faster.

When you begin to communicate with your A-Body, you can remain healthy wherever you are. Perhaps, you may have never communicated with your A-Body. We will understand how we can communicate with the A-Body and exercise its healing abilities in the next chapter.

5

Healing with the A-Body

We will now go through the steps of healing with the A-Body. Each part of your physical body has an A-Body. Every part, every organ of your body has its A-Body counterpart. The constituent A-Bodies together form your whole A-Body.

Consciousness is the point of reference

In order to communicate with the A-Body, it is first important to understand the reference point from where you are perceiving the A-Body. In other words, you have to be clear about who you truly are.

As we've seen earlier, consciousness is the Source of everything. It is the essence of our existence, our true nature. Our mental and physical bodies are a vehicle employed by consciousness to experience its essential nature and express its divine qualities such as love, joy, peace, creativity, patience and courage.

Consciousness is all-pervading. It is not just within the mind-body. Rather the mind-body is an expression within the field of consciousness.

The mind-body is an observable phenomenon in the field of conscious awareness. We are that conscious awareness.

Being conscious awareness, we can witness feelings and thoughts that arise as the mind and the sensations that arise as the body.

This standpoint has to be clear when you are seated to invoke and communicate with your A-Body.

Before you start healing through the A-Body, it is important to reiterate the understanding:

- Every disease and every disorder can be healed completely.
- A perfect blueprint of our healthy body always exists in the A-Body.
- The A-Body is capable of reproducing perfect health in the B-Body.

The perfect blueprint can be likened to an auric template that is present in the A-body. This template holds the characteristics of the perfect state of the body. When we communicate with the A-body and invoke its healing ability, we are simply restoring the B-body from its current state to its original perfect form. In other words, when the physical body resonates with the restored original blueprint, it gradually takes on a perfected state.

We will now go through the steps of healing with the A-Body.

Sit down in a relaxed posture with closed eyes and perform the following steps.

Step 1: Welcome

You address your A-Body by inviting it into your field of awareness. For example, suppose you are experiencing pain in the knee. You will invoke the A-Body of your knee.

'Dear Divine A-Body of my knee [or the ailing body part that you choose], I welcome you into my field of attention.'

It is fine even if you do not use these exact words. But the intention behind the words should be to welcome the A-Body of your knee into your awareness.

Step 2: Assert

In the second step, you revive the capabilities of the A-Body of the specific part by asserting its power.

'You have the power to heal yourself and the B-Body.

You can cure any ailment.

I have the power to cure myself.

Together, we have the power to even heal the world.'

You assert this with the conviction that the A-Body carries the perfect blueprint that can be reproduced to restore the healthy state of the specific part of the body.

When you assert, '*I have the power to cure myself,*' you are asserting from the standpoint of Self, the Source. It means that the Self has the power to dispel its lack of self-awareness and experience itself.

The last line, '*Together, we have the power to heal the world*' asserts the potential power of the Source and the A-Body to collectively heal the universe. You place a higher purpose, a higher vision, beyond the individual body and awaken the healing power for the larger cause.

Step 3: Act

After asserting the truth, you will give the A-Body an action plan. It is like reminding someone that he can accomplish a task and then asking him to act immediately. Instruct the A-Body thus:

'Now start healing yourself and your B-Body.

Continue to heal even after you have left my field of awareness.'

The A-Body is the manifestation of intelligence. You can dialogue with it, just as you would with your best friend. You can communicate with the A-Body to entrust the task, just as you would delegate a task to an intelligent person. You instruct the A-Body to continue the healing even after you are done with your dialogue, so that the A-Body progresses further with the healing later even when you are not consciously aware of the healing process.

Step 4: Allow

Love, joy and peace are three primary qualities of the Source. Here, love represents unconditional boundless love, which is beyond attachment. It is the power that creates and sustains the manifest universe. Joy is the unconditional bliss that transcends the polarities of happiness and sorrow. It is bliss that is felt simply due to existence, rather than any specific prerequisites. Peace refers to the pure stillness, which is the nature of existence at the core of one's being. It exists beyond the duality of noise and noiseless silence. Instruct the A-body to invoke the power of Love, Joy and Peace.

'Love, Joy and Peace have the power to enable healing.

Allow Love, Joy and Peace to work through you.'

Love, Joy and Peace have the power to enable healing. These qualities are always readily available. We unconsciously block them out from our lives due to our limiting beliefs. In this step, you instruct the A-Body to consciously allow Love, Joy and Peace to work through it and facilitate the healing process.

In order to invoke the qualities of Love, Joy and Peace, you will begin to chant and awaken their power of healing.

'Love, Joy and Peace are now helping the A-Body to become healthy.

Love... Joy... Peace...

Love... Joy... Peace...

Love... Joy... Peace...

...'

To the extent that you deeply feel the nature of Love, Joy and Peace, to that extent, they begin to manifest in your field of awareness and enable the healing. Give sufficient time for this invocation. Continue to chant at least for two to three minutes. With the repeated chant, only three words will remain: Love, Joy, Peace.

When you reduce words and focus your attention on a select few, you get into a state of relaxed focus. You stabilize your attention only on these qualities of the Source.

Step 5: Support

Invoke the A-Body of your brain to help by requesting it to relay specific healing instructions to your body part. You can instruct the A-Body of the brain to regulate breathing and facilitate proper blood circulation to the specific body part for purification.

You may have heard of phantom pains – pains that linger even after certain body parts like the leg are amputated after an accident. The reason for such phantom pains is that the sensory center for that part continues to relay signals in the brain, causing the false pain. You can now use the power of the A-Body of your brain to relieve such phantom pains.

You can also invite the A-Body of your hand into your field of awareness and request it to help your knee (or the relevant body part) in healing.

Touch or pat the body part gently and lovingly with your palms, as though you are putting a child to sleep. Even if it is an internal organ like the liver or pancreas, the hand can be placed on the skin over the relevant organ. If you have a headache, you can place the physical hand on your head and request the A-Body of your hand to help in healing.

Step 6: Sensory inputs

You can make use of the three powerful sensory modes – sight, hearing and touch to intensify your invocation of the healing process.

If you are naturally more visual, then you can use the power of visualization and picture divine white light bathing the specific part of your body that requires healing.

If you are predominantly auditory, then you can use the power of words by chanting a positive affirmation.

If you are kinesthetic (if your sense of touch and feelings are predominant), then you can gently touch the part of your body with your hands. You can thank and bless it.

Step 7: Gratitude

Thank all: the A-Body of the ailing part, hand, brain, and also your whole A-Body, which helped you in focusing your relaxed attention.

'I am grateful to you all…

I expect health miracles… I am open to health miracles…

Thank you… Thank you… Thank you…'

When you thank your mind-body, the feeling of gratitude helps in speedy recovery. The power of gratitude can set right disturbed vibrations and align it with the natural flow of the Source.

Having thanked the A-Body, you can then lovingly send back the A-Body out of your field of awareness.

'Please continue to heal even after you leave my field of awareness.

You may now leave my field of awareness. Thank you.'

With the seventh step of gratitude, you can remain in silence for a few minutes and then open your eyes.

A brief review

There is no need to be concerned about jumbling or forgetting the steps or missing specific words that were explained earlier. Understanding the purpose of each step is more important. What is the science behind it? What is the purpose? What does the assertion mean?

A brief synopsis of the seven steps of healing through your A-Body is outlined below.

1. Welcome

>*Dear Divine A-Body of my [the ailing body part],*
>
>>*I welcome you into my field of awareness.*

2. Assert

>*You have the power to heal yourself and the B-Body.*
>
>*You can cure any ailment.*
>
>*I have the power to cure myself.*
>
>*Together, we have the power to heal the world.*

3. Act

>*Now start healing yourself and your B-Body.*
>
>*Continue to heal even after you have left my field of awareness.*

4. Allow

>*Love, Joy and Peace have the power to enable healing.*
>
>*Allow Love, Joy and Peace to work through you.*

Love, Joy and Peace are now helping the A-Body to become healthy.

Love... Joy... Peace...

Love... Joy... Peace...

Love... Joy... Peace...

(continue chanting)...

5. Support

You may rally support from the A-Body of your hand to assist in the healing process. You may also invoke the A-Body of the brain to maintain proper breathing and blood circulation.

6. Sensory input

You may visualize white light bathing the ailing part, or repeat positive health affirmations, or even lovingly touch and pat the part with your hand.

7. Gratitude

I am grateful to you all...

I expect health miracles... I am open to health miracles...

Thank you... Thank you... Thank you...

Please continue to heal even after you leave my field of awareness.

You may now leave my field of awareness. Thank you.

Powerful assertions to assist in A-body healing

The following assertions can be repeated frequently to reinforce the understanding of the remedy:

- *No disease is incurable. The cure for any disease is within me.*
- *I know that every cell in my body is being renewed.*
- *The body which had the disease is no longer present.*
- *I only need to stop giving undue attention to the ailment.*
- *I expect health miracles in my life.*
- *I am now free from all disease.*

Research on application of A-Body healing

In a research survey conducted on a group of participants from various age-groups for a diverse range of diseases and disorders, 54% of the participants belonged to the age group between 25 and 45 years.

Of the diseases and disorders that were addressed, 100% participants experienced healing effects. While 74 participants tried the technique for aches and pains, healing was reported even for cases of hypertension and cardiovascular disorders, diabetes, headaches and also for swine flu.

The time duration for which the technique was applied varied depending on the specific disease. One-off aches and pains were found to be healed in an application duration of less than 10 minutes. Other diseases such as cardiovascular disorders, flu, gastro-intestinal diseases, diabetes required regular A-Body healing sessions lasting upto 10 minutes, repeated 2 to 3 cycles every day.

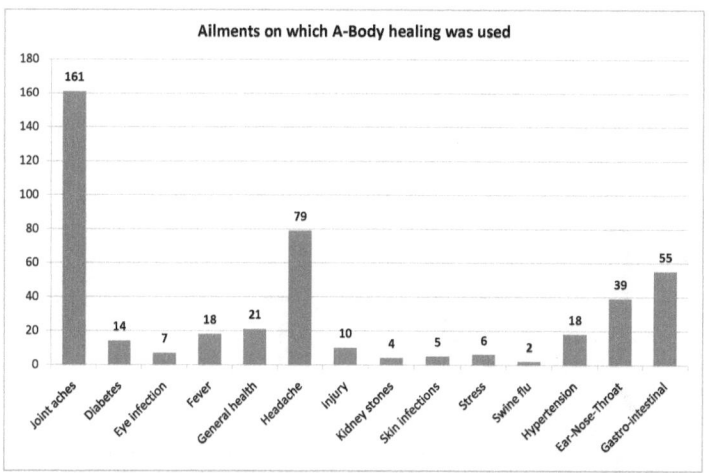

The research work also analyzed other treatment modalities that the participants were undergoing at the time of the survey. 61% of the participants reported healing only with the A-Body technique in isolation.

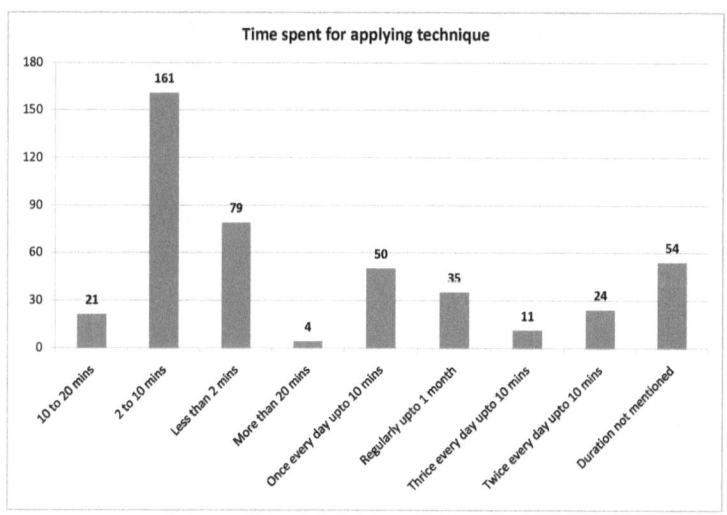

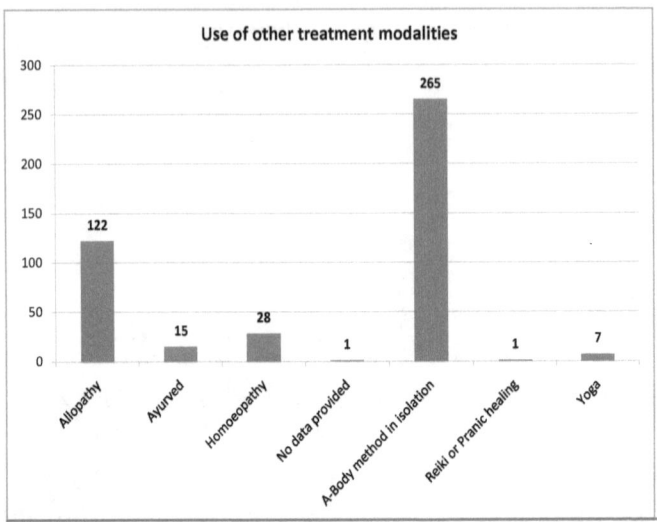

Patience and Persistence

Direct communication with the A-Body sets the healing process into motion. If your A-Body were present in a fluid non-physical world, then the healing intention that you communicate to the A-Body could cause instant transformation. The changes would be instantaneous and miraculous as the A-Body is not bound by time and spatial barriers of the physical world.

However, the B-Body is not as malleable as the A-Body as it belongs in the denser physical world. Hence, when you communicate with the A-Body, it could take time for the healing to be reproduced in the physiological and structural aspects of the B-Body. It could also be instantaneous in certain cases, but it could also take time in other cases.

Hence, patience and persistence are key to ensure complete healing.

We need to persist with our communication with the A-Body consistently till the healing shows effect on the B-Body.

To many people, this may seem to be too simple and illogical to be true. However, there are thousands of people who have practiced this and are reaping benefits.

Those who are suffering from ailments should communicate with their A-Body at least two to three times a day, if not more. Consistency and persistence are keys to success. Whenever you get the chance, communicate with your A-Body to experience the miraculous results that many are already experiencing.

6

Understanding and Dealing With Emotions

There was once a man who suffered from a very painful and life-threatening form of spine arthritis. When he was admitted to hospital after succumbing to paralysis, the doctor told him that his condition was so bad that he had very little chance of recovery. They tried every possible treatment but to no avail.

When traditional methods failed to improve his condition, the man left the hospital and checked into a hotel instead. He started watching hilarious movies and television shows, believing that laughter and positive feelings would do to him what medicine couldn't. He soon found out that just ten minutes of intense belly laughter was enough to give him two hours of pain-free sleep. This had not happened in a long time. Encouraged by the results, he kept firm belief and faith that he would recover. With the help of prayer, meditation, love and laughter, his health finally started improving.

What did this man work upon during this process? His feelings.

Every day, he examined the feelings arising within him. He was convinced that his feelings determine his health. He even started receiving proofs of this conviction in everyday life. Within a few months, he recovered completely and started living a healthy and beautiful life, for he was brimming with only positive, healthy feelings. He was none other than the famous writer, Norman Cousins.

Feelings like stress, anxiety, fear and anger have a debilitating effect on health. Researchers once conducted an experiment on three groups of rats. The first group of rats was kept in ordinary conditions and fed ordinary food. The average lifespan of this group of rats was found to be two years. The second group of rats was kept in stressful conditions and fed the same food as the first group. To create stressful conditions, a cat was tied next to their cage. This group of rats lived to an average of just six months. The third group of rats was kept in good conditions and fed healthy, low-calorie food. Most rats in this group lived for three to four years.

You can infer from this experiment that we need positive feelings like peace, love, and courage in addition to ideal food to keep good health.

What are emotions

The subconscious mind has been designed to automate responses to certain stimuli. Since childhood, we observe and learn certain fixed responses to external stimuli. The subconscious mind is the storehouse of such fixed responses. For example, we don't need conscious interpretation to pull our hand away from fire. The subconscious mind is automatically programmed to enact this response to the stimulus of fire.

Likewise, there are certain fixed responses that are triggered in various parts of the body from the subconscious mind when it encounters and interprets an input to match a stored response. For example, when we are cornered and threatened, depending on how we have been programmed during childhood, our subconscious may either trigger an emotion of fear or the emotion of anger. Various emotions reside in specific parts of our body.

- Arrogance resides in our joints, causing them to become rigid.
- Deceit leads to diseases of the throat and lungs.
- Stubbornness causes stomach ailments.
- Uncontrolled anger and irritability reside in the liver and gall bladder, causing ailments.
- Fear resides in the kidneys and the urinary bladder.
- Resentment or hatred resides in the lungs causing respiratory disease.
- Stress and worry reside in the pancreas, causing ailments thereof.
- Impatience and impulsiveness affect the heart and small intestine.
- Grief that is suppressed takes its toll on the lungs and the large intestine.

- Miserliness or greed express physiologically as constipation, malfunction of the sweat glands and the functioning of the lungs.

The destructive effect of emotions

Most people allow destructive emotions like hatred, sorrow, depression, restlessness, lack of faith, bitterness, anger, fear, worry, envy, stress, miserliness, resistance, and revenge to dwell in them. It won't be wrong to say that the reins of your health are held by your mind. A heart attack may very well turn out to be a 'hate attack' (attack by hateful feelings) or a 'head attack' (attack by negative thoughts).

A mind filled with anxiety can easily make one psychotic. The poison of anxiety slowly spreads in the body and makes it a lodging for disease.

Negative emotions drain all the enthusiasm from the mind and cause depression. People who are afflicted with depression for long periods even give up the will to live. Those who have no will to live take a long time to recover from illness. On the other hand, those who are eager and enthusiastic about living an interesting life recover quickly. They can win against the most fatal diseases.

Anger and stress create tension in the nerves, leading to pain. Such tension caused by anger can last from three hours to as many as three days. People who are prone to anger and stress even need to be prescribed sleeping pills. The solution is acceptance. Acceptance and happy feelings reduce nerve tension rapidly.

Before attacking its prey, a lion looks into the prey's eyes first. If it sees fear in the prey's eyes, it attacks immediately. But if the prey shows no signs of fear, the lion waits until the prey loses confidence. If the prey remains fearless even after a long time, the lion goes another way.

The same happens with disease and health. The lion in the above analogy represents disease. Disease inflicts those people who are filled with fear and negative emotions. But as soon as it sees healthy feelings like love, joy, peace, faith, goodwill, purity and abundance, it goes another way.

Every emotion seeks attention and release

Every emotion seeks to be understood. Whenever any emotion arises, it is as if the emotion is saying, "Please understand me." Every emotion arises to seek release, to be set free.

However, the subconscious programming that we have been handed out since childhood causes a feeling of discomfort. One tries to escape from the emotion, instead of witnessing and understanding what the emotion exactly is.

An emotion is like a child who seeks to be understood by its parents. The child may create a hue and cry to get attention. When parents are unaware of the deeper nuances of dealing with the child's real need, they either silence the child by scolding or stifling it, or provide the child with temporary diversions.

In the same way, man either shuts down the emotion by suppressing it, or finds some temporary way of escaping it by diverting focus to topics that provide temporary relief. This does not help in releasing the emotion.

Methods of handling emotions

People know of only a few ways to release emotions and most of these give only temporary relief. The need now is to understand the right methods to achieve freedom from emotions. Only then is it possible to rise to the highest level of health. But before talking about the right methods, let us talk about two wrong methods that people usually employ to get rid of negative emotions.

First method: Expressing the emotion on others

The first method commonly adopted by people to dissolve their emotions is spewing it out on others. This is a very dangerous method because it creates karmic bonds. Hatred, envy and anger ultimately lead you to burn in the fire of regret. Anger may arise due to any reason, but it always ends in regret and sorrow. The person we dump our negative emotions on, keeps looking for an opportunity to bounce back with a befitting answer.

If you feed sugarcane to a sugarcane juicer, the sweetness of the juice is experienced first by the juicer and then by others. Similarly if you feed stones to the juicer, it is the juicer that gets harmed first. In this analogy, the juicer represents our body; the sugarcane juice symbolizes positive emotions and stones symbolize negative emotions. You can understand from this analogy that if you shout an insult at someone, he may or may not be affected by it, but you will certainly affect your own health.

If one does injustice to others by expressing emotions of anger or resentment on them, then he may temporarily safeguard his physical health, however at the cost of harmony in his relationships. Others around him become vulnerable to his emotional outbursts.

Second method : Suppressing emotions

The second commonly adopted method is suppression of emotions and feelings. Someone who suppresses his feelings may appear calm on the outside, but actually he is simmering inside. When he can no longer bear his suppressed feelings, he suddenly explodes one day like a volcano that erupts when the earth cannot bear the pressure anymore.

If one suppresses the emotion when it is triggered, it makes matters worse. Sustained suppression leads to proliferation of physiological malfunction in the organ where the emotion resides.

Some people experience mood changes when seasons change. For example in the summer, some people feel apprehensive because they remember the time of their annual school exams. People are not able to lend the right expression to their feelings when their mood changes. They often keep their feelings suppressed. Suppressed feelings lead to various kinds of illnesses.

Beware of the two methods given above. To achieve freedom from negative emotions and feelings and rise to the heights of health, adopt the five steps given below.

Step 1 : Take advice from well-wishers

Open out and share your feelings with a trustworthy friend, relative or counsellor. Sharing your negative feelings with someone trustworthy, makes you feel light and relaxed. Sometimes, mere talking is enough to set free many of your negative feelings. The person you open up to also helps you by listening to you attentively and giving suitable advice.

In the initial journey towards complete health you can make use of this first step. But you need to move beyond this step as well. You may even write down your feelings. Writing down your feelings has the same effect as sharing them with someone reliable.

Step 2 : Encounter your feelings

You can make use of your intellect and encounter your feelings. For example, if the feeling of fear is troubling you, take it as a challenge and overturn it. If you are constantly worried whether you might be affected by some disease, encounter this feeling by asking yourself evincing questions until you get to the bare facts. For example:

I have worried about various illnesses in the past. Did all of them happen to me?

No, but some of them did happen.

Were they as dangerous or severe as I had feared?

Not all, but one or two were.

Was I able to tackle those one or two occasions?

Yes. It means I can tackle them in the future as well!

In this way you can utilize your power of logic and invalidate your emotions. But there is an even better method, the ultimate one, to get rid of negative feelings.

Step 3 : The ultimate method

The most effective method to become free from the grip of negative feelings is to view them as a detached witness. Emotions are like storms raging in the ocean. They come and go. Your viewpoint while the storm comes and goes is the most critical aspect of this method. If you alert yourself and raise your awareness in this time interval, you will learn the trick to detach yourself from the emotions.

The trick then is to neither express, nor suppress, but witness emotions from a detached standpoint.

Such detached witnessing has three aspects:

1. Understanding

When we observe our emotions, we may initially find it difficult to detach from them, as we are habitually identified with them. There is a deep notion within us which suggests that 'All this is happening with me.'

When we learn to abide in the experience of the Source, we gain conviction that we are neither the mind nor the body. The mind and body are expressions of pure consciousness that we essentially are.

When we do not have this understanding, emotions can be so overpowering that we may lose clarity of our true identity. Attachment to emotions leads to clouding of this understanding. Even to remember that this is "Not with me" can help in detaching from the emotion and connect with the alert awareness that is witnessing all this.

The other important truth that we need to be convinced about is the temporary nature of these thoughts and emotions. Who-we-truly-are is permanent, eternal. Emotions and thoughts come and go. They are like flares that shoot into the night sky. They appear for some time and then fade away in the sky of consciousness.

This understanding can be deepened by the practice of abiding in the stillness of presence. When we practice meditation to detach from our thoughts, body sensations, and emotions, we begin to become familiar with the constant background of awareness that is witnessing all these.

Emotions need to be witnessed with this detached standpoint of vigilant awareness, an undisturbed curiousness with the understanding that it is 'not with me'. Love and acceptance is naturally inherent in such witnessing.

When we resist emotions that arise, we energize and strengthen them. Witnessing emotions with love and acceptance de-energizes them and leads to their release.

Why do emotions get released when witnessed with love? It Is because, there is neither attachment, nor aversion in pure love.

2. Sameness

The other aspect of detached witnessing is a sense of sameness with which we perceive all emotions and thoughts. Sameness is about ascribing a value of alikeness to both painful and pleasurable emotions. A perspective of evenness where there is neither a like nor a dislike for what is being witnessed.

Superficially, emotions like anger, depression, or resentment will appear to be very heavy and intense. The subconscious programming triggers an instant impulsive reaction by giving an exaggerated weight to the emotion.

When we slow down and watch the emotion with an attitude of sameness, we are able to question the weight of the emotion. What may appear to be a heavyweight emotion, of the order of 50 kg, will then turn out to be not even 5 grams. This is the revelation that can result out of deep observation with evenness.

3. Alertness

Being vigilant is essential to remain detached. When we are not alert, the natural tendency is to identify with the stories and their associated emotions. We need to have an alert awareness that is uncompromisingly focused on itself. It vigilantly utilizes emotions and thoughts that arise as hooks to defocus from what arises and focus on our essential Presence.

Step 4 : Giving a positive expression to your feelings

No incident is troublesome in itself; it becomes troublesome only when you describe it with negative words. Whenever an incident happens, most people may describe it according to their state of mind at that moment. They choose some words for describing their feeling at that moment, like "I am feeling scared… I am feeling insecure… I am shocked… I am fed up… I am worried… I am depressed… I am very angry… I am so restless…" etc. Thus they choose certain words for describing each feeling. The irony is that they most often choose negative words.

If you choose the word 'worried' for your feeling, this word will trigger further worry. Hence, don't label the feelings arising in your body. Simply view the tension, muscle contractions, changed vibrations, etc. as they are and tell yourself, "Like every incident, this incident has come to teach me something by presenting me with a challenge. The solution to this problem lies hidden in the problem itself. I need to discover it and use it as a ladder for progress. I will definitely get the fruit of overcoming this challenge."

Step 5 : Determine the worth of each incident

Suppose you go to a shop to buy a matchbox and the shopkeeper is selling a 50 cent matchbox at ten times the price. You won't buy it, because you know that the shopkeeper is asking for more than it is worth.

We need to adopt the same approach to deal with life's incidents. If you happen to be upset with a trivial incident, it means that you may be paying more than it is worth. For example, suppose you were to get wild at someone when you came to know that he has spoken ill about you. Without validating whether it is true, you may waste your mental energy and harm your health for a trivial reason.

These five steps to handle emotions will help get rid of them and develop divine qualities like self-discipline, courage, power of discrimination, patience, a flexible intellect, and mental stability. You will experience wonder, love, joy, peace and complete health. Our feelings affect not only our physical health but also our efficiency, creativity and productivity.

Part II

The Law of Health

7

The First Law of Health

Your mother is suffering from stage 3 cancer," announced the doctor to Samir.

Samir was shocked, "Oh no, Doctor… how can this be?"

"Look Samir, your mother has only a few days left. I suggest that we do a surgery to extend her life."

Saddened, Samir trudged out of the hospital. He could see only gloom descending before his eyes. Samir was very attached his mother. After his father had passed away, his mother had taken good care of him and brought him up amidst testing circumstances.

The doctor's words were causing him great anguish. As soon as he went home and informed his mother about her cancer, he began to cry like a child. Surprisingly, there was no trace of sadness on his mother's face. Samir was astounded to see her courage.

As the days went by, Samir grew more and more desperate. The doctor's words kept ringing in his ears. He would wake up in the middle of night and worry about his mother's imminent demise. His thoughts turned negative, becoming grim by the day.

One morning, Samir woke up and stayed in bed for a long time recalling sweet memories from his childhood. With teary eyes, he thought to himself, "How I wish my mother had more days to spend with me! I want to take her on a pilgrimage. I want to do everything that I can for her."

He sprang to his feet, boosted by these thoughts. He resolved to brighten the last few days of his mother. Just then his mother called out to him and said, "Samir, my child, I know how worried you are. I can see that you are not able to stay focused on your work. Let me tell you something – I firmly believe that I am going to recover. I want to recover completely and I am sure that I will."

Samir was stunned. His mother's words gave him goosebumps. Looking at her silence for the past few days, Samir had assumed that she would have resigned to her fate. But now he could see the spark in his mother's eyes. He could feel the strength of her will to live. He now realized that she had not spoken a single negative word ever since she had heard about her cancer. She had maintained a calm composure and prayed several times with folded hands.

Finally, the day of her surgery arrived. Samir's hand trembled as he signed on the consent form. He was clearly scared. He waited patiently outside the operating room. After two hours, the doctor stepped out. There was a smile on his otherwise solemn face. He pronounced to Samir, "This is probably one of the rare cases where a stage-3 cancer has been completely cured in first attempt!"

'What do you mean, Doctor?' asked an anxious Samir.

"Samir, this is indeed a miracle! Your mother has no trace of cancer in her body. I have treated hundreds of cancer patients before. But not a single third-stage victim has ever survived. Your mother is the first one to recover from such an advanced stage of the disease. I didn't find a single tumour in her body! Today is one of the most memorable days ever in my career!"

Samir was overwhelmed with delight. He couldn't control his tears, though this time they were tears of joy. When he met his mother, she was still praying with closed eyes and folded hands, "I am absolutely fine. I am healthy."

Have you heard or read about such incidents before? Medical science has seen many such cases of spontaneous remission from terminal illnesses that evoke awe and wonder. Yes! Even so-called incurable diseases surrender before the might of thought. The power of thoughts can create miracles. It can dissolve even the most stubborn of diseases.

Everything in the world is first created in thoughts, whether it is recovery from an incurable disease, experiencing happiness, or attaining the fruits of prayer, or the sight of a disabled person standing up on his own legs without support. If you desire excellent health, you need to see it in your thoughts first. You need to believe in it with complete faith. This is the First Law of Health.

The first law of health simply states:

Before manifesting in physical form, health is first created in the realm of thoughts from the Source.

Nature says 'Amen' to each one of your thoughts, whether positive or negative, whether healthy or diseased.

Evidences that thoughts influence matter

It is the most obvious truth that thoughts influence our body. When you get the thought of holding this book to read it, it triggers neurons in your brain to execute movements of your hand muscles in a coordinated manner so as to hold this book. All physical actions through our bodies are actually wondrous examples of how thoughts regulate the body.

However, most medical practitioners, until recently, have not considered mental factors while diagnosing disease. Their primary focus is on biochemical aspects. They attempt to treat disease by effecting chemical changes in the body.

There is unquestionable evidence that has proven beyond doubt that our thoughts are largely influential in determining our physical wellbeing. Some of these are mentioned here:

1. Experiments with water

In a groundbreaking experiment, Dr. Masaru Emoto and his associates exposed water samples from various sources to a variety of spoken words – both positive and negative expressions. They also exposed water samples to a variety of music – both harmonious and jarring. Subsequently, they froze the water samples and photographed the crystals that were formed in frozen water.

Water samples exposed to words like 'Love you', 'Peace', and 'Thank You' formed beautiful hexagonal crystals. However, water samples exposed to words like 'Fool' or 'Hate you', 'You make me sick' produced malformed and fragmented crystals.

This experiment provided concrete visual evidence of how water reacted to both positive and negative energy.

The average human body is made of 70 percent water. Throughout our physical lifetime, our bodies exist mostly as water. Since we are made primarily of water and since water can be influenced by positive and negative energy, it becomes all the more vital that we re-look our thoughts and feelings. Our attitudes can directly impact our whole being including physical health.

2. Placebo effect and spontaneous remission

You might have heard of people becoming healed after taking a sugar pill or following a procedure that convinces them of wellbeing. This is a common phenomenon, which is known as the placebo effect. It is a direct result of your mind believing that you will get better even if the treatment was faked.

The placebo response is one of the most fascinating manifestations of the body's self-healing capabilities. It is the result of partnership between a mind that believes in the effectiveness of a given treatment and the body that fulfills the expectations of the mind by exercising its inbuilt healing intelligence.

Also, there are cases reported of people suddenly getting healed from cancer and other terminal illnesses, merely because they have had a profound change in their beliefs or outlook towards life. Such cases are known as spontaneous remission.

These phenomena are demonstrations of the functioning of the

First law of Health: Before manifesting in physical form, health is first created in the realm of thoughts from the Source.

A study conducted on a group of medical students showed that they had a diminished immune system functioning at exam time. Students also reported higher incidents of coughs and colds during their exams.

The two emotional factors that adversely affect health are stress and grief. Through medical studies, it has been discovered that heightened emotional states can stimulate the spleen, an organ that plays a major role in the immune system.

Unfortunately, most people, being ignorant about these things, tend to be caught up with their negative emotions and allow anxiety, anger fear, sorrow, and guilt to interfere with their health. They continually dwell in negative thoughts about themselves and the world.

Our health is determined by our beliefs

Certain behavioral instincts like the child's instinct to swim when placed in water are fundamental to our survival and inherited through DNA. For example, we are born with the ability to swim. Infants can swim gracefully after they are born. But children learn to fear water as a result of the forbidding by their parents due to fear for their safety. Our learned perceptions and beliefs override our genetically programmed instincts and begin to rule our lives.

This learning starts not just after birth, but even earlier in the womb. Neuroscientists and psychologists are now finding evidences that fetuses and infants rapidly feel and learn from their environments even when they are in the womb. The mental and emotional disposition of parents plays a vital role in influencing the learned beliefs of the child even before its birth. It determines our long-term health and behavior. These learned beliefs also predetermine our susceptibility to various diseases like diabetes, obesity, hypertension etc. in later life.

However, the same learning faculty becomes less effective when the children cross the age group between 6 to 10 years. This is because the chatter of thoughts based on programmed beliefs occupies most of the mental activity of the conscious mind.

To re-program our beliefs, we will need to still the chatter of the conscious mind at least to some extent, so that new beliefs can be impregnated into the subconscious mind. It is essential that we learn to access the experience of the Source and dwell in the stillness of pure consciousness. This makes it conducive to re-program our subconscious mind with wholesome thoughts.

While most of our behavior is determined by preconceived beliefs held in the subconscious mind, it is also receptive to instructions received from the conscious mind.

If we consciously entertain negative thoughts about health, it only reinforces negative beliefs in the subconscious mind leading to manifestation of disease. For example, someone who has got a respiratory infection in winter may have harboured a notion during childhood that winter is time of sickness time for them. If they happen to catch the virus again during a later winter, their notion is reinforced into a belief. With repetitions of such instances, the belief becomes imprinted in their physiology, so that they dutifully falls ill at the onset of winter.

Psychosomatic disorders are physical diseases that are caused or made worse by our negative beliefs. Illnesses like ulcers, irritable bowel syndrome, asthma, eczema, psoriasis, hypertension, heart disorders and even cancer are strongly influenced by negative beliefs held in the subconscious mind.

If negative limiting beliefs can cause disease, then positive thoughts can be used to our advantage to restore health. Upon close observation, you'll find that there are two kinds of people: the first are those who are brimming with health, while the others are those who invariably tend to fall ill. What is the difference between these two kinds of people?

The first kind of people have the reins of their health in their own hands. They have mastery over their lives. Life seems to flow easily for them as they intuitively know and apply certain laws, even if they cannot put them into words. They are able to stay calm with faith in the power of their thoughts, even if they encounter diseases.

The second kind of people are those who are constantly in a state of struggle. They choose to be victims to circumstances and give in their health to self-defeating beliefs, being rid with illness and negativity.

It is not just health that is created in your mind first. Your capabilities, your success or failure, the people coming into your life, your financial situation and the incidents happening in your life are all created in your mind first. Only then do they manifest in visible form.

Let's go back to the earlier story. In spite of suffering from cancer, Samir's mother consistently dwelled only on one thought with full faith: "I am healthy… I'm at the pinnacle of health… I'm going to be perfectly fine." What she focused on became her reality. Her affirmations bore fruit and she attained complete health. It is important that we should have firm faith in our affirmations. To assist in developing firm faith, dip into the experience of the Source for a while through prayer or meditation before reiterating your affirmations.

Today, studies in mind science have proved that programming our subconscious mind with healthy and wholesome thoughts revitalizes every cell in the body even while we sleep. We first need to plant the seeds of health in the subconscious mind, and it manifests in the body later. In spite of this reality, most people like to think and speak about sickness and pain rather than health. In doing so, they shut out the healer within them unknowingly.

Hence, to protect yourself against negative thoughts and their effects, arm yourself with the understanding of the laws that govern health and transform your thoughts. If you simply change the way you look at thoughts, your life can undergo a wondrous transformation. This is because your world (which includes your body) begins to change as soon as your perspectives and beliefs change.

There was a person who had begun feeling uncomfortable and weak since some days. He had begun to lose weight. He was consumed with the belief that he was suffering from cancer. He was so convinced that he visited the doctor and insisted on diagnostic tests to confirm his doubts. The doctor organized a complete health check and informed him, "None of the reports suggest cancer. I've checked them thoroughly." The person still continued with his doubts, "But Doctor, I've heard that there are certain types of cancer wherein the symptoms don't show up. Perhaps I may be suffering from some such cancer."

It would be no surprise if this person invites death through his own thoughts. The power of thoughts is so immense that it can help you fully recover from incurable disease or even lead you to untimely death.

Thus, if you contemplate on the first law, you will realize that your physical health is a reflection of your mind. The thoughts that you constantly reiterate have a corresponding effect on your body. If you keep positive thoughts, they revitalize every part of your body. Each one of your thoughts is associated with certain groups of cells in your body. By transforming your thinking into a positive one, you can activate cells in the brain, spine and muscles to regain health.

You need to make changes in the world of thoughts and feelings in order to see changes in the world. Your health is in your hands. The only need is to understand and implement the laws that govern health.

8

The Second Law of Health

In the previous chapter, we have seen that thoughts affect our health in some way or the other. But we get countless thoughts each day, most of them may be insignificant or fanciful. Do all of them turn into reality? No.

The second law of health states:

Only those thoughts that we empower with awareness and enthusiasm turn into reality and affect our health positively.

The first aspect of this law is awareness. We need to bring presence and clarity to our thoughts. Most of the time, we lose ourselves in random thoughts. One moment we want one thing and the next moment we want another. We either dwell in thoughts about the past or fantasize about the future. We worry, we fear, we greed for things. In such a commotion of thoughts, we mostly veer from what we really want towards negativity.

If you are not getting what you desire, the primary reason for it is that you haven't empowered your thoughts with awareness. If you start doing so, very soon you will see miraculous results. Why have so many people today slid into illness? Because, there is no clarity in their thoughts and they don't believe that it is possible to achieve health. Their random thoughts work against each other and become totally void of potency. Hence, pause and reflect on your thoughts from time to time. Check whether they are nullifying each other.

An ill person thinks, "It would be so nice to get rid of this illness completely!" This thought immediately sets into motion nature's creative process of sending him the fruit of his prayer. But the next day he thinks, "But if I get well, I will have to start helping with the household chores again. I will also have to go to work again. It is so exhausting! I'm so happy to relax at bed right now. Everyone is taking care of me. They are serving me great food, fruits, juice…"

This is how thoughts nullify each other. We don't realize the damage that we inflict upon ourselves through negative thoughts. All that was ordered through positive thoughts doesn't reach us because the order was cancelled through negative thoughts.

People sometimes wish for good health and sometimes fear that they might die young since they don't exercise at all. Their thoughts of fear nullify the power of their prayers for health.

It is essential to be aware of the laws of thought and have faith in them. Trust the potency of your thoughts enthusiastically and plant seeds of health consistently through consciously directed thoughts. Else, the mind can drift into aimless fantasies which never come true. If your thoughts are devoid of awareness and enthusiasm, they stray in different directions and lose their potency.

Start programming your mind with healthy affirmations. If you repeat consciously chosen affirmations of health with faith, enthusiasm and awareness, they surely reach your subconscious mind. Your subconscious mind will then work on its own to attract health in your life. At minimum, be aware, not to harbour negative thoughts about health.

Most people are not aware of the laws of health. If they move two steps ahead with positive thinking, they go back two steps with negative thinking. Thus, they remain at the same place all their life. Even though they wish for good health, a minor headache is enough to send them spiralling down the abyss of negativity.

With the understanding of the first two laws of health, it is important to remain positive even when you are passing through a period of illness. Tell yourself, "This is not an illness; this is just the preparation for great health... These are mere clouds of illness that keep coming and going. Behind these clouds shines the eternal sun of health." Thus, empower your positive thoughts and vigilantly avoid contradicting them with negative self-talk.

If you feel that you are always positive regarding health and yet are not attaining it, it is time that you take a closer look at your thoughts. There is surely something that is contradicting your desire for health. Your positive, healthy and happy thoughts are being negated by some inner belief or hidden desire. You can uncover it only through honest contemplation. Be truthful to yourself and eliminate the belief that is pulling you down. Once you eliminate it, you'll be on the freeway to health.

Once you declare to yourself that you want great health, nature immediately begins the creative process. Then if you inadvertently wish to remain unhealthy in order to stay in bed, nature begins this process as well. It doesn't differentiate between positive and negative orders. It simply says 'Amen' to each one of your orders.

Everything is first created in thoughts, but it gains the power to manifest from strong feelings of passion and enthusiasm.

Sometimes, you don't see the results of what you wished for, even though you were very clear in your thoughts. Your awareness and clarity of thoughts do begin attracting the results towards you, but they struggle to reach you because you didn't empower your thoughts with enthusiasm. Since this is invisible, you don't realize that the results have stopped midway in their tracks. Tired of waiting, you stop empowering your thoughts.

For example, suppose in the pursuit of health you begin with positive steps like exercising well, eating only healthy food, praying and meditating. But yet, you go through a minor illness. If you become discouraged due to this illness and stop infusing your mind with enthusiasm, the health that was on its way to you halts in its tracks.

Only those thoughts that we empower with awareness and enthusiasm turn into reality and affect our health positively. The first aspect – awareness – comprises of clarity of thoughts and conscious direction. The second aspect – enthusiasm – comprises of intensity of will and persistence.

9

The Third Law of Health

When someone is ill, their family and friends visit them with flowers or fruits to wish them well. But do they really wish them well from within? Although nobody would intentionally wish

ill of the patient, some people do hold negative thoughts which they unknowingly utter, thus influencing the patient. Instead of getting well, the patient's condition becomes worse due to the demotivating words that reach their subconscious mind.

There are many who unknowingly feed the patient's mind with negative thoughts by making pitiful remarks like, "Oh! Why has this happened to you all of a sudden!? You were fine yesterday... Poor you! You have become so weak... Look at those dark circles below your eyes... Life is so unpredictable these days... our neighbour was of the same age as you; yesterday he felt uneasy just like you while he was on his morning walk; by evening he was no more..."

Instead, you can tell the patient, "You're looking great today...

you appear fresher than earlier!" You may talk about the last time you or someone else you knew recovered quickly from a similar ailment. It's even better if you can discuss the laws of thought with them to instil faith that that they can attract health with the power of thoughts. If you encourage the patient with positive words, their thoughts will work in the right direction and help them heal. They might also realize that the actual illness lasted only two days, but they remained languishing for many more days due to ignorance of the laws of thought.

When we fall sick, our mind often starts grumbling. However, grumbling only worsens the situation. Instead, we need to focus on happiness and health so as to get rid of the sickness quickly. If we happily set our focus on health, no illness can trouble us for long. Most people focus on what they don't want in life. Hence in accordance with the laws of thought, they end up getting those very things that they wanted to avoid.

So, in order to let the laws of thought work in favour of your health, affirm and empower the third law of health:

Focus on health, not on disease.

Each one of your thoughts works like a command; nature fulfils it. Hence be sure to focus only on thoughts of health. If negative thoughts about disease occur, let them pass. Do not empower them with your attention. This is the key to health.

Complete health is available to be experienced by each one of us. Instead of thinking "I don't want to fall sick," tell yourself, 'I am becoming healthier'. Let the habit of focusing on the positive rather than the negative become a part of your attitude towards life.

An experiment was once conducted at a military hospital where severely injured soldiers were brought to this hospital for treatment. At the entrance of a ward, there was a placard which read: 'Nobody has ever died in this ward.' Injured soldiers used to be in a negative frame of mind when brought to the hospital. Many of them would be counting their last breath. But as soon as they would read what was written at the entrance, all their negative thoughts would vanish, giving way to a glimmer of hope.

You can imagine how a string of positive thoughts must have run through them, due to which they could recover and go home. This is how the power of thoughts can pull someone out of the clutches of death and give them a new lease of life. Inspiring thoughts have the potential to transform your life.

Just as a single positive thought is enough to give new life to someone on their deathbed, so too is a single negative thought enough to bring disease, if not death, to a healthy person. For example, suppose a person who is drinking a glass of water is told, "Hey… a lizard had fallen in the water." If he is weak-minded, he may mistake any minor physical discomfort as a symptom of poisoning. He may possibly become seriously ill.

Vibrations and the Power of Focus

Each one of our thoughts creates its own unique vibration. Whatever resonates with this vibration gets attracted to your life. If your thoughts create vibrations that resonate with prosperity, prosperity comes in your life. If your thoughts create vibrations that resonate with peace, peace comes in your life. Similarly, if you create vibrations of love and health through your thoughts, you receive the wealth of love and health.

Anything that matches your vibration not just enters your life, but also grows many times over. The easiest way to benefit from this law of nature is to leverage the power of focus. Focus on what you want, and your vibration will naturally match it. With the power of focus, you direct your attention, and consequently your mental energy, towards it, and it will begin to grow steadily. This is just like watering a plant. The plant that is watered grows steadily while plants that are neglected wither away. Everything needs energy to grow, and by focusing on the thing you want, you provide it with mental energy.

Check where you are spending your valuable mental energy. Where are you investing your attention? Are you investing it in health, or sickness? Remember that you will receive whatever you focus your attention on whether it is positive or negative, desirable or undesirable. You will not only receive it but also multiply it several times over.

Hence, always be aware of your thoughts and let them focus on what you want – health, fitness, happiness!

What to do when sick

We all know the importance of physical health. We always try our best to avoid falling sick. We drink clean and pure water, we eat fresh fruits and vegetables, we maintain cleanliness of the body regularly, we have timely meals and we exercise regularly. Despite all these precautions, we do fall sick at times because the fear of falling sick still resides in our mind. We feel anxious and uncertain about our health. This automatically places wrong orders with nature. Nature simply fulfils them.

When we tell ourselves "I don't want to fall sick," images of the hospital, doctors, medicines, injections, etc. flit across our minds. Unknowingly, we place an order for such things with nature. As a result, we fall sick and receive all that we ordered for. We then keep wondering why we fall sick in spite of taking precautions.

Now, what is to be done after falling sick? You need to tell yourself,

"This is just a temporary little pimple of sickness; otherwise I'm always healthy." At times, you get a pimple on your otherwise clear face. But you don't worry about it, because you know that it is temporary. Similarly, you don't have to worry if you go through illness. Free yourself from the stress by reminding that it is temporary. Else, if you habitually focus on pain, weakness and boredom, you could be prolonging your stay in bed.

Focus on health-boosting affirmations

If our focus is on sickness, how can we expect good health? Focusing on negativity invites more difficulties. Many of us tend to focus our attention on negativity by thinking along the following lines:

- When will this sickness go away?
- Will I suffer from this disease?
- How will I lose weight?
- Will I suffer a heart-attack?

- Will I fall sick when the season changes?
- There is no guarantee of life, no matter how healthy you are.
- There is a wave of viral infection in town. Hope I don't catch it.
- No matter how hard I exercise, my weight keeps increasing.
- I was out in the rain yesterday. I think I might catch a cold today.
- Nowadays heart-attacks strike even at a young age.

These were only a few examples of negative thoughts that people generally keep repeating about sickness. Do you relate with any of them? By indulging in such thoughts, the feeling of fear grips the mind. Fear directly affects blood circulation in the body. Improper blood circulation weakens the muscular and skeletal systems. Gradually the body gets affected and you start feeling listless. The only way to avoid this is to focus solely on health and wellness.

If you want to abide by the Laws of Health and achieve good health permanently, be watchful of your mind and identify negative thoughts as soon as they pop up. You are now aware of the first law of health: Before manifesting in physical form, health is first created in the realm of thoughts from the Source. Hence, be alert and intensify only positive thoughts of wellness. Ignore and let go off negative self-talk. You can keep repeating some of the following affirmations. Repeating these affirmations can potentially bring about health miracles.

- Health is my birthright, and I shall enjoy it.
- I am healthy and powerful forever.
- I love to exercise daily.
- My enthusiasm and wellness are improving with age.
- I am always in favour of health.
- I have a strong stomach; it can digest anything.
- My health is an inspiration for others.
- With every breath, I am becoming healthier.
- My face radiates health.
- Divine energy is charging every cell of my body.
- Every day, in every way, I am becoming more and more healthy.
- I am tuned to health bulletins. I don't miss a single health update.
- My body is undergoing a miraculous transformation.
- My body is fit, strong and efficient because of balanced intake of food, regular exercise and a peaceful focussed mind.
- My body is a temple of consciousness and I am brimming with health, vitality and energy.

Consider connecting to the stillness of the Source before repeating these affirmations. Repeat these health-boosters whenever you are free. You may even record them in your own voice and listen to them any time at any place you please. Once your mind gets programmed with positive thoughts, you will begin to see miracles every day.

If you wish to exercise every morning but are unable to gather motivation to do so, repeat this affirmation with faith before going to bed at night: "Tomorrow I wish to get up early morning and enjoyexercising." This affirmation will be even more effective if you specify the time and duration: "I wake up at 6 every morning and exercise for an hour. It gives me immense strength, endurance and good health."

If you are unable to have your meals at the right time due to a busy schedule, tell yourself, "I am enjoying wholesome meals at the right time." If you repeat this affirmation in full faith with passion, you will automatically find yourself free to have your meals at the right time.

Imagine and experience the final result

Jai enthusiastically joined a gym. For the first few days, he used to get up at six, workout at the gym, have a healthy protein breakfast, and spend the day enjoying his newfound vitality. He was obsessed with the desire to develop good health. He worked out vigorously for a week. But after a week, he stopped going to the gym. Can you imagine why?

Jai had begun to experience soreness due to his workout. His focus had shifted to the aches in his muscles during the day. He was becoming restless. Fed up of the pain, he stopped exercising.

We often make the mistake of focusing on interim difficulties instead of the final result. Whenever you start exercising or following a healthy lifestyle, always focus on the final result. Imagine the final result and live that experience right now. Imagine that you have already achieved it and feel the happiness right now. Instead of focusing on pain, Jai should have focused on the fit and healthy body he would have achieved in few weeks.

Due to ignorance of the Laws of Health, we lose sight of the final result and quit the activity due to interim difficulties. Whether it is exercising, or following a healthy diet or developing positive self-talk, the moment it becomes a bit difficult, we quit. If we are suffering from a disease, we curse our fate and lament not being able to do whatever we could do before. Instead of looking up to the future, we wallow in sickness. This habit of focusing on the negative can potentially lead to sorrow. This is where the third Law of Health comes handy.

If you are suffering from some illness and trying to get rid of it, affirm to yourself with self-belief and happiness: "My body is brimming with health and strength." If you are unable to walk due to a health condition, repeat to yourself: "I am completely healthy and walking tall without any support." Imagine and experience the final result. Even if you do this for a few minutes, it may help immensely in your speedy recovery.

To quickly achieve your aim of health, make use of the power of your subconscious mind. Apart from words, the subconscious mind understands the language of images very well. If you wish to develop the habit of exercising daily, you can put up pictures of people who are working out and appear fit. This will send the right commands to your subconscious mind, helping in developing your habit of exercise. Even before the alarm rings every morning, you will find yourself up and running. In this way, make use of actual or mental imagery to reprogram the firmware of your subconscious mind.

If you are working out to lose weight, worrying about excess weight will work against your endeavour. Instead, feed your subconscious mind with images of exercise and healthy food. Visualize and admire the fit and healthy body that you will soon achieve. This will bring about more effective results.

Convince your mind about what you really want

Look at yourself in the mirror and say with a smile, "I am becoming slimmer and fitter. This lard of fat is melting away!" Be light-hearted about your weight and poke fun at it. This will loosen the negative grip that your excess weight has on your mind. Be jovial and let your mind relax. The positive flow of energy will drive you to success.

You cannot lose weight without first convincing your mind. People who wish to lose weight always use the term 'weight-loss'. But with the understanding of the power of words, we'd rather use the term 'health-gain' instead of 'weight-loss'. The positive goal of gaining health will naturally result in weight-loss as well.

People who are obsessed with either losing or putting on weight, lose focus on their overall health. Also, the word 'loss' creates a negative image in the subconscious mind. Most of the contribution to losing your weight comes from your beliefs. Hence, look into the mirror and tell your body, "You're doing very well. I am feeling light, healthy, fit, strong and agile because of your efforts… Thank you so much!"

The third law of health – 'Focus on health, not on disease' – is a secret that will unravel your possibilities for all-round health. When you abide by this law in daily life, you will reap the benefits of a healthy, fit, strong and agile body and a focussed and peaceful mind.

10

The Fourth Law of Health

In the social ecosystem which we are a part of, our lives are driven by our interplay with people around us. Very often, people are held with the belief that their lives are largely determined by others around them.

Many times, we feel that other people or situations are obstacles in our lives. Most people tend to squarely blame people around them for situations in their lives. You would have heard people saying, "If only this person were to change, all my problems will vanish". Perhaps you would at times, have thought this way.

Your interactions and behaviour with people have a telling effect on your health. Complete health encompasses not just physical health but mental and social health as well. The feelings and thoughts that arise during your daily interactions with people have a corresponding effect on various facets of your health. Hence it is but essential to understand the fourth law of health:

The facets of your health are a reflection of the state of your mind.

The underlying principle of this law is: *The world is not as it appears to you; the world is how you are. The world is a reflection of the feelings and thoughts you harbour about the world.* The world resonates with your feelings and thoughts.

Your complete health is an integrated result of your physical, mental, social, financial and spiritual states. These are facets of your health. Your social health is determined by how you relate to people around you, not just externally, but within your beliefs. Your financial health is governed mainly by whether you resonate with abundance or with scarcity.

If you hold a grudge that people don't help you, understand that the world is simply reflecting this belief of yours. Due to a few incidents in the past, you may have developed a belief that people don't help you.

Suppose people behave rudely with you, it is not necessarily because you behave rudely with them. It may be because you hold negative perceptions about them. Nature magnifies your assumptions and beliefs by a big factor before reflecting them to you through the world.

During your school days, you may have observed that students remain silent during one teacher's class but create mayhem in some other teacher's class. What could be the reason? The prime reason is the nature of thoughts running in the teacher's mind. The first teacher is happy and comfortable with the students. She thinks, "These kids are nice and well-mannered." As a result, the students are attuned to her and attend to her lessons. In contrast, the second teacher thinks, "Look at these spoilt brats... overindulged by rich dads...' Consequently, she is not able to establish a respectful relationship with her students.

It is easy to gauge the mental and social health of the two teachers in the above example. The one who has loving thoughts will definitely enjoy much better health than the one who has hateful thoughts. Thus you see that the outside world is a mirror that shows you your inner world, the world of your thoughts and feelings.

The thoughts and feelings that you transmit to the world are amplified and played back to you through the world. It helps to bear this in mind before grumbling about health. Whether you keep positive thoughts or negative, nature will send them back to you multiplied many times over. Nature doesn't differentiate between good and bad, health and sickness. It simply does its job of germinating the seeds you sow and giving you hundreds of the same fruit.

If you sow seeds of goodness, love and faith, you will reap its bounty. If you establish healthy relations with someone, nature will present you with hundreds more. If you spread health-boosting thoughts, nature will give your health a greater boost. Similarly, if you engage in hatred, resentment, anger and other negative feelings, they will be returned to you many times magnified, drastically affecting your social, mental and physical health.

Many people keep grumbling and complaining throughout the journey of life. They keep blaming their family, colleagues and friends for their failures. They are ignorant of the fact that the world is merely a screen on which you project your unresolved emotions, shortcomings and mental constitution. The images and movies you see on the screen are nothing but your own story. Just as we use a mirror to see our face and remove its blemishes, we need the world to witness our mind and remove its flaws. This is an extraordinary arrangement through which the Source works in our lives.

Forgiveness - the ultimate panacea

To unlock the highest possibility of health, you must get rid of all kinds of negative self-talk. The secret of getting rid of negative self-talk and achieving physical and social health simultaneously is *forgiveness*. The mind is covered with the dust of hatred, anger, fear, jealousy and other negative feelings. Forgiveness is the most effective way of removing this dust and giving an unobstructed way to supreme health in all facets of life. Forgive yourself, forgive others and, more importantly, seek forgiveness from others in order to get rid of negative feelings and thoughts.

You may mentally address those people for whom you have held grudges or entertained negative feelings. Mentally welcome their presence into your field of attention and inwardly tell them:

If I have hurt you through my feelings, thoughts, words or actions, please forgive me.

Please forgive me for not recognizing and honouring the Source within you.

I will take care not to repeat this mistake.

By seeking forgiveness, I am only doing a favour upon myself by releasing all negative feelings.

Thank you for this opportunity.

If you are comfortable meeting people face to face and seeking their forgiveness, you may do so. You can do this at least with close ones. Direct talk can bring instant results. When you seek forgiveness face to face, the clouds of hatred, anger, suspicion or guilt which are muddling your relations disperse instantly. When your mind becomes free and light, the health within you begins to shine forth.

Suppose you think you are not at fault in a broken relationship, and the other person too is not ready to yield. To prevent matters from worsening and to bring back the sweetness in the relationship, you can afford to take the initiative and apologize. It is probable that the other person will realize their mistake and apologize too. Their ego will melt when they see you apologizing for no fault of yours. Thus, forgiveness prevents a molehill from becoming a mountain and frees everyone from negative feelings and their ill-effects on health.

If you apologize and seek forgiveness from the world for your negative feelings, thoughts, words and deeds, and if you also forgive the world for its own negativity, then your social health will improve greatly.

If somebody is not ready to forgive you, don't consider their verdict as final. They are not saying 'No'; take it as if they are saying 'Not now'. Wait for some time and seek forgiveness again when the situation is favourable. This will release him from the clutches of hatred.

If you feel awkward about seeking forgiveness from people face to face, you can do so by sitting in meditation and communicating with them at the mental plane. Your feelings will definitely reach the subconscious minds of those you are communicating with.

Let us enjoy the benefits of health through the prayer of forgiveness as explained below.

1. Seeking forgiveness from ailing body parts

When emotions are suppressed, they are stored as unresolved memories. These memories are brought alive when relevant situations recur. They manifest at the mental plane as tendencies that make us react impulsively. These unresolved memories also manifest at the physiological level as diseases and disorders in various parts of the human body.

Due to ignorance of how this works in the unseen, most people cling on to negative feelings, inviting disease at the mental, physical and social planes. These wounded memories act as unseen strings of bondage that keep pulling us back and block the free flow of love, creativity, abundance and harmony in our lives.

Forgiveness is the ultimate panacea to cleanse such unresolved memories and resultant tendencies. It erases the impressions that cause bondage and clears the blocks that prevent free flow of life.

Seeking forgiveness from your body parts can heal diseases and disorders. As discussed earlier, every part of the body has its A-Body counterpart. Suppose one of your body parts or organs, let's consider the stomach, is in pain. Close your eyes and mentally communicate with the A-Body of that part as follows:

Dear divine A-Body of my stomach,

I invite you into the field of my awareness.

I have unnecessarily burdened you due to my wrong eating habits and worry.

You have suffered a lot. Please forgive me.

I am grateful for your unconditional service throughout life.

Hereafter, I will never do anything that causes you trouble.

You have the power to heal yourself. Please begin to heal yourself now.

Please continue to heal yourself even after leaving my field of awareness.

I expect health miracles.

Thank you very much.

2. Forgiving people who hurt you

By forgiving people who may have hurt you, you are liberating yourself from the bondage of negative emotions that you have held within. By doing so, you are only letting go of disease and opening yourself to a healthy life.

Every situation arises in our lives to teach us vital lessons. They help us mature. Even seemingly hurtful incidents are actually opportunities to weed out our negative impressions and respond creatively from a standpoint of higher awareness. Though this may appear farfetched in the heat of a given situation, we can be grateful for incidents in life that may appear to be hurtful, for they actually help us learn our life lessons and truly grow.

In a meditative state, connect inwardly with those who have hurt you in the past and say:

Dear divine A-Body of _____,

I invite you into my field of attention.

I am now letting go of all the hatred, bitterness and complaints that I have held about you.

I forgive you in the presence of _____ as a witness #.

I love you and respect you.

I reacted without recognizing and honouring the Source within you.

I held negative feelings about you by considering you to be an individual person.

I failed to see the divine consciousness in you.

I am sorry for this. I will not repeat this mistake.

I am now in favour of Love, Joy and Peace.

Thank you for giving me the opportunity to learn and grow.

3. Seeking forgiveness from people you hurt

You may have perhaps hurt some people in life, knowingly or unknowingly. If you have done so, you have caused karmic bondages. One by one, mentally bring each one of these people before your mind's eye and communicate inwardly with them:

> Dear Divine A-Body of _____,
>
> I invite you into my field of awareness.
>
> In the presence of _____ as a witness [#],
>
> I sincerely apologize for having hurt you through my thoughts, feelings, words or actions.
>
> I dealt with you as if you were an individual person.
>
> I didn't recognize the divine consciousness in you.
>
> I sincerely seek your forgiveness for this.
>
> I will try my best not to repeat this in the future.
>
> Thank you for being in my life!

Reconcile the day's dealings before sleep

Seeking forgiveness as described earlier will help eliminate karmic bondages caused by reactive behaviour between you and others. It is a good practice to pray for forgiveness every night before going to bed. Recall every incident that happened since morning and check whether you felt anger or hatred for anyone. If so, forgive and seek forgiveness with a big heart. Pray for the wellbeing of all those people who triggered negative feelings or thoughts within you.

We shouldn't ignore a single karmic bond, whether strong or weak. If you leave any feeling unresolved, it will bother you the next day as well. A housekeeper wipes the kitchen clean every night so that

---

[#] Invoke your Higher Self, Guru, God or anyone whom you hold in deep reverence, as a witness to your forgiveness.

she doesn't have to deal with rotten garbage when she returns next morning. She doesn't wish to waste her time, mood and health dealing with yesterday's trash. Like the housekeeper, make a habit of cleansing your mind every night before going to bed.

When practiced sincerely from the bottom of our heart, these prayers of forgiveness will bring a feeling of lightness. It will fill your heart with love. When you wake up next morning, you can spread love to everyone around you. When this is practiced every day, very soon you will see great results. You may be amazed to see previously rude people speaking politely with you, your relationships blossoming, your healthimproving. You will begin to feel lighter and more peaceful than ever before.

Deep rooted illnesses will begin to lose their hold on you. You will be able to heal them effortlessly. But all this first begins to manifest in the invisible realm. Hence, you shouldn't be discouraged if you don't see immediate tangible results. Keep faith that the practice of forgiveness will definitely lead to tangible and wondrous results.

To usher complete health, we should stop focussing on others' shortcomings. Instead of investing our attention on others' blemishes, we can utilize it for unfolding our own creative possibilities.

The following prayer can help in achieving physical and social health. You can say this prayer every night at bedtime.

I forgive all those who have hurt me knowingly or unknowingly today.

I release them from any binding created due to my feeling hurt.

I sincerely seek forgiveness from all those whom I may have hurt through my thoughts, feelings, words, or actions today.

Please forgive me for not recognizing and honouring the Source within them during my interactions.

I seek forgiveness from the parts of my body that I abused.

I will try my best not to repeat this in the future.

By doing this, I am not doing a favour on anyone else, but myself.

I am raising my purity of mind and elevating my level of consciousness.

I am transforming my own vibrations and enriching my life with love, joy, peace and health.

Thank you for giving me the opportunity to learn and progress.

11

The Fifth Law of Health

Nature has everything in abundance. Countless flowers blossom every moment. Mother Earth produces countless fruits, plants and grains every year. If you sow one seed of marigold today, you will see hundreds of marigolds blooming in your garden in a few months. Within each flower lie hundreds of seeds. Anyone can count the seeds in an apple, but can anyone tell how many apples are there in a seed?!

The starry sky is home to billions of galaxies like ours. Can we ever measure the water in the ocean? Can we count the number of medicinal herbs in the world? There are countless flowers whose extracts can cure various kinds of diseases. The principle of abundance applies to each and every aspect of creation in nature.

The question is – if everything in nature is available in plentiful supply, why do we see a lack of health on Earth?

Many of us live with a mindset of scarcity. We hear many people complaining, "I don't have this… I should have got more… How can I do with so less? Water scarcity is becoming so rampant in our region." By repeating such self-talk, people sink deeper into the mindset of scarcity. But nature is capable of providing for everybody's needs and more.

There are a countless variety of species of fish, mammals, plants, algae, etc. living in the ocean, even deep down on the ocean floor. Yet, all their needs are fulfilled in the ocean itself. If nature can provide for life that ranges from microscopic algae to mammoths like whales, can't it provide for each one of us as well?

The fourth law of health states:

Everything, including health, is available in abundance for everyone.

Love, happiness, wisdom, health, wealth, the company of caring and industrious people, success, virtues… everything is abundant. When it comes to health, rest assured that it is available in unlimited supply for everyone on Earth. You can get everything you want, because nature has far greater reserves than any individual can ever need. Nature is like an ocean from which you can draw any number of buckets of water. No matter how much water you take out of the ocean, it doesn't reduce the ocean. This applies to health too.

Most people find it difficult to have faith that they can enjoy good health because their focus remains on the lack of it. They protest inflation of prices and complain that good food and medicines are not affordable. They grumble about the degrading quality of foodstuff due to use of toxic chemicals in agriculture. They worry about the quality of medical services. They rue the lack of time for exercise. All of such negative self-talk points at scarcity.

Such people feel fatigued all day long because the thought of inadequate sleep remains at the back of their mind. They miss their schedules, they don't have their meals on time and they don't exercise regularly.

The feeling of abundance relaxes every cell of the body. Besides health, qualities like love, happiness, peace, prosperity, wealth, and creativity are all abundant in nature. Health is the nature of nature! The only need is to feel the presence of abundance. It is because of disbelief in abundance that people fall victim to various kinds of diseases. Our judging and rational mind cannot believe in nature's laws even though we are fully capable of expelling diseases. When children fall down and injure their knee, the injury heals within a matter of a few days. But injuries that happen to adults generally take a longer time to heal. The speed of cell regeneration reduces with age due to the onset of negative beliefs. Scary thoughts can delay the process of healing.

During deep sleep, your conscious mind is silent, but your subconscious mind remains active. In fact, the subconscious mind is active twenty-four hours a day. Consider a child who falls asleep while playing with his toys. His mother then comes and puts all his toys in order. When the child wakes up in the morning, he finds all his toys organized tidily. Similarly, when you go to sleep amidst troublesome negative thoughts, your subconscious mind works on these thoughts. With careful observation, you'll find that you generally wake up with the same feeling that you had while falling asleep. Hence, be watchful of your thoughts while going to bed. Always keep yourself motivated with positive thoughts before sleeping. It is a very good habit to pray for forgiveness and repeat health-boosting affirmations before lying down. This will ensure that you wake up fresh and motivated in the morning.

When your thoughts are in harmony with the principle of abundance, you will attain good health in all facets of life. People of miserly nature tend to be unhealthy as they act against the principle of abundance. Due to their belief in scarcity, they are always apprehensive of giving. It is a law of nature that you reap in multiples of whatever you sow. Water from the ocean evaporates, travels inland in the form of clouds, falls in the form of rain, and returns to the ocean in the form of rivers. Though the ocean gives in a carefree way, it never experiences shortage of water because everything is abundant.

Those who have a miserly nature are very likely to suffer from constipation because they have the habit of holding onto even unwanted things instead of giving them away. They feel restrained while spending. Their closets are filled with things they haven't used for years. They tend to store things, only to feel secure. As a result, their subconscious mind signals their intestines to hold onto waste. Such people need to repeat the following affirmations:

'I am secure because I know that everything is abundant.'

'I happily let go of unwanted things from my body and mind.'

'I believe in abundance, not in shortage.'

Divine plan of health

The law of abundance can also be referred to as the divine plan of life. Everyone on earth is born with a divine plan of abundance. It is an arrangement by nature. The plan unfolds abundance and prosperity in your life, only if you can decipher it. Everything in nature is easy, straightforward and abundant. With the knowledge of the laws of health, you can easily reach the summit of your possibilities on earth. The feeling of scarcity is not in harmony with the divine plan. This feeling blocks your way towards the summit. Hence, keep faith in the principle of abundance and start implementing it… right now.

Nature is a complete source of health

Each one of us has a unique physical constitution. One may feel fresh after eating eggplant while another may feel sick. Some may find bananas nutritious while others may find them difficult to digest. But nature has a fruit for each one of us. A fruit consists of many parts like the flesh, seeds, skin and juice. If some fruit does not suit you, it doesn't mean the whole fruit is bad for you. A single fruit has so many aspects to it. If you find it difficult to digest a banana, try eating the fibre pulp stuck on the inside of the peel after eating the banana. You can see that nature provides a remedy in the same fruit that causes you trouble. This is the way of nature. Nature is complete in itself; it is a complete source of health. You only need is to believe this and experiment.

There is ample time for health

Many people complain of lack of time for exercise and healthcare. Actually, what they lack is not time, but the effective management of time. Such people tend to eat their food so quickly that they are unable to digest it properly. They gulp down their juice or milk instead of enjoying its taste. Such people cannot achieve complete health because their mind is busy racing and complaining, 'Where is the time?' This feeling of shortage prevents them from exercising, eating food slowly, enjoying the taste, taking adequate rest and other such healthy habits.

Instead of entertaining thoughts of shortage of time, you can think light and happy thoughts like, *"There is abundant time available. I am learning to effectively manage my time to make the most out of it."*

If you are among those who feel the shortage of time for exercise, perform the following experiment. Suppose you want to exercise for half hour every day, at least five days a week, then write down:

- Days in a week = 7
- Number of hours in a day = 24
- Number of hours in a week = 168
- Minimum number of exercise days = 5
- Duration of exercise per day = half hour
- Therefore, the total weekly duration for exercise = only 2.5 hours or 150 minutes

When we look at this closely, we realize that there is ample time available for exercise. Dedicating only 2.5 hours out of 168 for physical vitality should be easily possible. If there is any inadequacy, it is only in the thinking, which is influenced by the belief of scarcity.

If you wish to build your muscles by working out in the gym, have faith that nature is providing you ample support. The muscles that you exercise in the gym are replenished and strengthened in the next 48 hours. Hence always tell yourself, "I have ample support from nature for achieving my health goals."

Remember the exceptional rule of nature: You receive whatever you give, multiplied many times over. If you give time, money, help, love, attention, appreciation, food, or knowledge, nature gives it back to you, multiplied many times over. But if your focus is on receiving, it only suffices your sustenance. Take advantage of this law of nature and invest your time and attention towards developing your health.

Rational thinking leads us to believe that we can prosper only when we receive. But the law of nature is contrary to this. The intellect may find it difficult to reason how you can prosper by giving, rather than receiving. But you can experience it for yourself only by following this law. You may have already applied this law before, but perhaps unknowingly. Whatever progress you have made so far in the physical, mental, social, financial or spiritual facets of your life is a result of giving. And you can give only what you have. This is another law of nature. When you give the thing you have, nature returns it to you in multiples.

Believing that health is abundant helps us harmonize with nature. Prosperity is the quality of nature, and we are part of nature. The more we attune with nature, the more we open ourselves to intuition for the steps to improving health.

Some questions for your contemplation:

1. Am I focusing on scarcity instead of abundance? Am I focusing on sickness instead of health?

2. What is the negative limiting self-talk that I unknowingly keep repeating due to which health has halted in its way towards me?

3. Am I prepared to give time, money, help, love, attention, appreciation and knowledge to others?

12

The Sixth Law of Health

There was a frail man who was constantly ridiculed for his poor health. Whenever he tried to exercise to build his body, people would ridicule him. Even his own family used to abuse him because of his frail health and frequent illness. Nobody cared to motivate him. Out of dejection, he consulted a psychologist. He explained how people bullied him whenever he was about to take a new step towards health. He complained about his friends and family, blaming them for his weak health.

The psychologist looked at him for a while and said, "Bring me a small bucket of water." The man was surprised but followed what was told. The psychologist poured the water into three vessels and placed them on the burner. When the water came to a boil, he put a carrot in the first vessel, an egg in the second, and some tea leaves in the third.

After some time, he removed the three vessels and let them cool down. He turned to the person and said, "Take the carrot and tell me how it feels." The person took the carrot, felt it and said, "It has softened." The psychologist asked him to peel the egg and feel it. The person did so and said, *"The egg has become firm."* Finally, the psychologist asked him to sip some tea. The person poured the tea, sipped it and smilingly asked the psychologist, *"What is this all this about?"*

The psychologist explained, *'The carrot, the egg and the tea leaves, all faced the same adverse situation... boiling water. But each one reacted differently. The otherwise firm carrot softened and became weak. The usually weak egg protected by a frail shell stiffened. And the dry tea leaves transformed the water into tea."*

He continued, *"Who are you? Are you like the carrot that appears firm but weakens in testing situations? Or are you like the egg that becomes hard and stiff upon facing trials? You can also be like the tea leaves that spread their fragrance when they are put to test; they transform a seemingly negative situation into a positive outcome.*

He advised the person, "People may taunt and ridicule you. But whether you get affected by them or not is entirely your choice. Suppose I place a hard stone in boiling water. Will it affect the stone in any way?"

"Not at all," replied the person, *"because it is solid and unyielding."* The psychologist said, *"If you decide to become solid, unyielding and unshakable like the stone, no situation in life can trouble you."*

How you react to what people think about you is your choice. Your mental state reflects in your physical health. If you choose to maintain a strong and positive state of mind in any situation, you can enjoy good health. The story throws light on the fifth law of health.

Others' negative thoughts cannot affect your health unless you allow them to.

Nobody has the power to make you fall sick. Whether they curse you or think ill of you for whatever reason, your physical and mental health depends solely on your own thoughts. Unless you allow your thoughts to be influenced by others, your health remains firmly in your own hands.

Those who are unaware of this law borrow negative opinions from others. Due to lack of faith in health, many people indulge in ramblings like: "Nowadays, there is no guarantee of life beyond sixty years", "Life has become so fast-paced that it is impossible to remain healthy", "People aged above forty years must take preventive medication for high blood pressure", "Heart attacks are not restricted to seniors; these days youngsters in their twenties can also suffer heart attacks," "No matter how much we care for our health, it is ultimately at the hands of fate", "Energy and enthusiasm reduce with age", "The weather is so fickle nowadays; it is easy to catch a virus," and so on.

Negative thoughts program the subconscious mind, which in turn affects every cell in the body. Suppose someone remarks, "You are looking weak and frail nowadays. Is something wrong?" Now it is up to you whether or not to allow this remark to affect you. If you keep thinking about it and validating the remark by looking at yourself in the mirror, you program your subconscious mind accordingly. Thus, you unconsciously choose to become weak and frail by giving attention to such remarks.

Instead, if you become alert and aware when you hear such negative remarks, you can make use of it in whichever way you please. You can choose to remain unaffected like the stone in the earlier analogy, or positively transform it like the tea leaves by telling yourself, *"I am absolutely hale and hearty. I am brimming with health, energy and enthusiasm!"*

If you are with someone who thinks ill of you, their thoughts cannot affect you directly. But since they can affect you indirectly, be aware of your own thoughts and don't let them sway in the wrong direction.

Suppose you are with someone who thinks negatively, not just for others but also for themselves. Their thoughts may attract matching results for them, but not for you if you maintain awareness. Suppose you are driving a car and your co-passenger is paranoid about meeting with an accident. If you are unaffected by their thinking, you will not attract an accident. Even if they were to verbalize their fears constantly, alerting you to be careful and narrating their tales about road mishaps, you can still remain unaffected by remaining focused on positive thoughts. But if you are affected and begin to worry, you might attract an accident.

You might have heard people complaining, "We are suffering the karmic results of others' deeds… It is because of them that this is happening to us…" According to the fifth law of health, this can be an indirect consequence, not a direct one. If you start thinking negatively without being fully aware, you might attract matching results.

You need to ensure that you never fall victim to negative thoughts floating around. Be assured that without your permission, nobody's negative thoughts can affect your health. Unless your own thoughts veer in the wrong direction, your health will not be affected.

The effect of brainwashing is also visible in the case of women's health. For many centuries until recently, women were subdued and restricted to household activities. They were made to believe that they are weaker than men. They were always discouraged from performing heavy physical activities and pursuing adventurous hobbies. As a result of centuries of negative programming, women actually started believing that they are physically weak and frail.

Some women are so strong and healthy that they can beat men in any physical competition. Women have scaled Mount Everest; they have won weightlifting competitions, they have beaten men even in wrestling matches. Why are some women able to achieve what most women consider impossible? This is because they are unaffected by negative talk going around. They don't allow others to influence their thinking.

Advertisers also play a big role in influencing your thinking. Since they want to push their products, they create a sense of false fear in people's minds. 'Pop this pill to prevent cold…', 'Use these supplements to avoid brittle bones…', 'Use this toothpaste or else suffer from cavities…' Such barrage of illness-related commercials cause unwary viewers to sow the seeds of illness in their minds. We should learn to be detached from newspaper and TV commercials.

There are many who get affected by negative and pessimistic suggestions, making their lives a veritable hell. Being subject to people's criticism, ridicule and negativity, those who are weak-minded invite diseases. We need to heed this law and be aware about the ultimate choice of health, which is our birthright.

The path that leads to the pinnacle of health – mental, physical and social – exists within us. Our health does not depend on any doctor, dietician or psychologist. These practitioners are available to help us, but ultimately the reins of our health lie solely with our thoughts.

13

The Seventh Law of Health

Sam was diabetic since the last twenty years. One day, he finally decided to take charge of his diet and lifestyle.

With all earnest, he started daily exercise, proper diet, total abstinence from sugary foods, and regular checks for blood sugar.

For about fifteen days, Sam religiously followed a strict regimen. But his tower of resolve collapsed when he became a grandfather. The celebration was cause for his indulgence in sweets and carbs. His blood sugar rose to the same high as before.

This may resemble the story of many of us. Sam wanted to get rid of diabetes completely. He had an intense desire to do so and there was adequate clarity in his thoughts as well, thus aligning one of the laws of health. But his compulsive actions deviated from his chosen path. Had his actions been aligned with his feelings and thoughts, he would have immediately become wary when he saw his favourite dishes laid out on the table.

This calls for understanding the seventh law of health:

To attain and sustain complete health, your feelings, thoughts, words and actions must be in alignment.

The law explains that even though we may have noble intentions, we may not always have similar thoughts. What we do may contradict what we say. This lack of integrity in feelings, thoughts, words and actions results in nothing at all. A visionary had once said, "*The biggest illness plaguing the modern world is the enormous dissimilarity in people's thoughts and deeds.*"

One may feel very motivated to follow a health regimen, but at the level of thoughts he or she has not generated the clarity of how and when to do it. Their words may be constantly describing illness and their actions may be sporadic. There are many people who can give a vociferous half-hour speech on the importance of exercise, but when the timer rings at six in the morning to remind them to jog, they snooze the timer and convince themselves that they will start the next day. Despite knowing that tomorrow never comes, they don't make an effort to get their act together. They don't think what they feel, they don't say what they think, and they don't do what they say. This lack of integrity in feelings, thoughts, words and actions gives rise to disease.

Let us understand this law with the help of an example. Suppose you want to wake up early every morning and go to the gym. What should your feelings, thoughts, words and actions be like?

Feelings: You need to be enthusiastic. Before going to bed, you need to look forward to waking up early, feeling fresh and energetic, and setting out in the cool morning air. If you go to sleep with such a feeling within, you will wake up on your own before it's time. You will most probably not need an alarm.

Thoughts: Before going to bed, you need to think about exactly which exercise you want to perform next morning in the gym. If you don't make up your mind, then in spite of getting up early, you may probably spend time in unnecessary thoughts. Before going to bed, you must also prepare yourself to get out of the cozy warmth of your bed as soon as you wake up in the morning. If you don't think it through, you might want to stay snugly wrapped in the blanket for some more time, ending up missing your workout. It is important to pay attention to every thought, because even one can derail you from the journey towards health.

Words: Your feelings and thoughts will help you wake up on time. Now you will contribute with your words as well. You will appreciate your efforts and say positive things about them. You would avoid contradictory words like, "Is it really necessary to wake up so early? My friends are always late to the gym; let me sleep for some more time. Is exercise really going to help?" Words like these can make you change your decisions at the eleventh hour.

Actions: Action is the final cog in the wheel of success. Your feelings, thoughts and words may be in harmony. But to set the wheel in motion, you need to take suitable action as well. Consider keeping your jogging shoes or gym bag right beside your bed so that they are the first things you see when you wake up in the morning. When you wake up, push aside the blanket in which you were snuggling and jump out of bed immediately. Upon getting up and freshening up, immediately start preparing for the gym. Pack your things, change into gym wear, wear your sport shoes and set off. If you don't take immediate action, you might sink into your sofa and start reading the newspaper or watch TV. Lack of suitable and immediate action allows procrastination and lethargy to set in, ultimately foiling the grand plan you make for health.

Feelings, thoughts, words and actions are the four essential cogs in the wheel that rolls towards the destination of health. Even if one cog is missing, you will not reach the destination. Most people tend to neglect one or more of them. As a result they go nowhere in spite of making a lot of effort.

It is important to work on all four dimensions together. Imagine, you have to remove a screw from a wall. The screw has penetrated so deep into the wall that even its head is not seen.

You need four things to do this job. You need a nail to hit from the other side of the wall so that the head of the screw can be seen from the side where it has gone in. You need a hammer to hit that nail. You need a screwdriver to unscrew it once you see the head. You need cutting pliers to pull the nail out.

The problem is that most people only use one tool – say the screw driver or cutting pliers. Some just even do not use a tool – they try pulling it out with their bare hands. The result is that the nail either does not come out or it may come out clumsily, damaging the wall, after eons of effort. The smoother way is to use all four tools together - one after the other.

If your thoughts and feelings are negative, your words and actions will also be negative. And therefore the results will also be negative.

If a diabetic feasts on sweets and says that he doesn't want the consequences of his actions, this won't happen. If this person wants to get rid of diabetes, he or she will need to change his actions. To change his actions he will need to change his words. And to change his words he will need to change his thoughts and feelings.

Behind the thoughts arising in the mind is the power of feelings. Thoughts can take shape only with the help of this power. When a particular thought becomes firm, its effect is seen in our words and behaviour. Our action is based on our behaviour. Results are the consequence of our actions. So, the key lies in our feelings.

Feelings are the foremost aspect of this law. Dr John Albert Schindler has said that three out of four patients admitted in hospitals are victims of EII. EII stands for 'Emotionally Induced Illness'. In scientific terms, these are called psychosomatic diseases or disorders, i.e. diseases or disorders caused by mental factors. Dr. Schindler's research proves how prolonged depression sets off negative responses in the nervous and endocrine systems, producing symptoms of disease.

Emotions translate to biochemical events in our bodies. Researchers from the UK have found evidence that depression doesn't just change our brains, it can also alter our DNA and the way our cells generate energy. A study conducted on a selected group of subjects who had stress-related depression - associated with some kind of adversity during childhood, it was found that the energy needs of their cells had changed in response to stress. They were more prone to fatigue and anaemia. It's becoming increasingly clear that our emotions also affect us on a biological level.

We must pay special attention to our feelings. If you have negative feelings about your health, then your thoughts, words and actions will also reflect this negativity. So take control of your feelings. Affirm to yourself, "I want complete health. I want to be brimming with energy and wellbeing." Then your thoughts, words and actions will follow suit. Once again, assert the seventh law of health: To attain and sustain complete health, your feelings, thoughts, words and actions must be in alignment.

Now, please keep this book aside and contemplate for a minute – what feeling do you have about your health right now? Do you really wish for whatever this feeling will ultimately create in your life?

If your feelings align with what you truly wish in life, then immediately lend support to your feeling with suitable thoughts, words and actions. If not, then immediately change your feelings.

If you infuse your mind with feelings of good health, resultant thoughts will follow and your body will prepare itself to take commensurate action – like working out, having balanced meals, meditating, avoiding junk food, etc. Thus, feelings are the starting point and thoughts, words and actions fall in line thereafter.

It is seen that those who are always positive about their health are the ones who exercise regularly without fail. Such people don't consider exercise a burden. In fact they are always eager to boost the 'feel good' hormones in their bodies. 'Feel good' hormones are beta endorphins that are released by the pituitary gland when you work out intensely. These hormones relax the entire nervous system, making you feel good. This experience programs your subconscious mind to love exercising. Your body and mind become tuned to the idea of regular exercise. Your thoughts, words and body language also begin to reflect this positivity. Consequently, all the four aspects of the seventh law– feelings, thoughts, words and actions – align in the same direction and propel you to health.

Many people constantly nurture negative feelings such as fear, hatred, jealousy, depression and vengeance. Such feelings give rise to negative thoughts, which in turn express as words and actions. Biochemical events in the body turn negative and bring about disease in every cell. Let's take a few examples to illustrate this fact.

1. The feeling of fear affects the digestive system and causes related illnesses.

Feeling : Fear

Thought : "What will happen now…?"

Words : "I'm afraid of this…"

Effects of biochemical events: Stomach ache, change in appetite, change in body weight, appendicitis, restlessness, insomnia, hair loss, intestinal gas, bedwetting in case of children, diarrhoea, peptic ulcers.

Peptic ulcers are a result of excess fear and inferiority. Some people keep thinking, "I do not deserve good things in life…", "How can I face this problem?", "I'm not capable of fulfilling my manager's expectations…", "I am not a good parent…", "I am not a good partner…". The feelings behind such thoughts are fear, insecurity or inferiority. People who harbour such feelings and thoughts express the same in their actions. Such people keep inflicting their subconscious minds with treacherous blows. The negatively programmed subconscious mind sends matching signals to the intestines. The stomach produces excess acid to cope with the stressed intestines, resulting in peptic ulcers.

Health affirmations to transcend this condition:

I am courageous. My capability is improving day by day. I have faith in life. I am safe and secure.

I believe in courage, not fear.

I love my healthy diet and lifestyle. I am relaxed and peaceful.

2. An inflexible or stubborn mindset can lead to stiffness or pain in the neck, back or joints.

Feeling: Conceit, inflexibility

Thought: I am always right. People should listen to me.

Words: Mark my words!

Effects of biochemical events: Stiffness and pain in the neck, or back or joints.

Health affirmations to transcend this condition:

My feelings, thoughts, words and actions are becoming flexible and accommodating.

Everyone is right from his or her point of view.

Now I can easily see the various aspects of any given thing. I can easily bow down to the ones I love.

3. Constant feeling of guilt or resentment arising from thoughts of unpleasant incidents in the past may lead to body pain, depression, disinterest, muscle stiffness, constipation and backache.

Feeling: Guilt, Resentment

Thought: 'I shouldn't have done this.' 'They shouldn't have done that.'

Words: 'I deserve to be punished for my deeds.' 'The other person deserves to be punished.'

Effects of biochemical events: Listlessness, body pain, stiffness. A lot of people are unable to forget the mistakes they made in the past. They keep recalling painful memories and complicating them with new thoughts. Such people are likely to suffer from muscle stiffness, tumours, cancer and urine stones.

Health affirmations to transcend this condition:

I fully accept my past.

I forgive myself for all the grudges that I have held onto. I forgive everyone and let go of the past.

I love myself unconditionally.

Things that I don't need are easily going away from my life. I easily let go of unwanted memories.

Only pleasant memories remain with me.

4. Feeling of shortage and inadequacy maylead to perpetual fatigue and improper sleep.

Feeling: Shortage, inadequacy

Thought: 'This is not enough for me.'

Words: 'I never get what I want.'

Effects of biochemical events: Fatigue, constipation

Health affirmations to transcend this condition:

Everything is abundant – love, happiness, peace, wealth and health. Health, security and prosperity are available in abundance to me. Abundance is my nature.

Staying healthy is easy and straightforward because it is my nature. Health is my birth-right.

5. Nurturing anger, irritation, hatred and worry could lead to acidity, migraine, high blood pressure, heart ailments, diabetes and back pain.

Feeling : Anger, hatred, worry, irritability

Thought : 'I don't like this person… I cannot tolerate this… I don't like that…'

Words : 'My blood boils when I see this person.'

Effects of biochemical events : Acidity, migraine, high blood pressure, heart ailments, diabetes, back pain.

Worrying about the future affects the blood circulation system, leading to heart ailments and high blood pressure. People suffering from anxiety are unable to envision a happy picture of their future. Such people are even prone to eyesight disorders.

Health affirmations to transcend this condition:

I love everyone. Everyone loves me.

I am free from hatred and brimming with love.

Stability is my nature.

I am carefree, happy and peaceful.

I forgive everyone and also seek forgiveness.

These were just a few examples that indicate the consequences of negative feelings and thoughts on health. You may use these to look within and identify the negative feelings and thoughts that may have perhaps led to your physical illness. After identifying them, replace them with relevant health affirmations.

This does not need you to delve deep into the causes of your negative thoughts or feelings. Your focus should largely remain on positive affirmations, because it is your focus on positivity that will transform your inner feelings. When your feelings become positive, your thoughts, words and deeds will also become positive, and health will become your nature.

Part III

The Tools for Health

14

The First Tool – FOCUSED SELF-TALK

Recent scientific research directly or indirectly explains how affirmation techniques work to effect self-healing. There is evidence that the human DNA can be influenced and reprogrammed by words and frequencies without the need for intervention in the physical plane.

Only 10% of our DNA is used for building proteins. Till recently, the other 90% was considered "junk DNA." However, nature cannot create something that is redundant. Recent collaborative research by linguists and geneticists to explore this 90% of "junk DNA" has resulted in findings that are revolutionary. According to them, our DNA is not only responsible for constructing our bodies but also serves as means for data storage and communication.

It was discovered that the apparently useless 90% of the human DNA contains encoded data that follows the same grammar rules of syntax and semantics as our human languages. So the evolution of human languages is not a coincidence, but rather a reflection of our inherent DNA. Due to this, human DNA resonates with human language.

So it turns out that we can use words and sentences of human language to influence living DNA! This has been experimentally proven. DNA present in living tissue responds to language-modulated inputs.

This scientifically explains why affirmations and autosuggestions have such strong effects on our bodies and physiology. Spiritually evolved humans have known for ages that our body is programmable by language, words and thought. This is now gaining scientific ground.

Without this knowledge, most people unknowingly keep repeating negative words and statements for themselves because they do not realize that our speech, mental and spoken, deeply impacts our minds and bodies. When these thoughts are repeated over and over again, they turn into deeply rooted beliefs that have negative consequences on health.

The Power of Affirmations

I am the embodiment of complete health.

I am becoming better and better with every passing day.

If you repeat this affirmation consistently, your body-mind mechanism gets programmed for experiencing complete health. When the body-mind mechanism accepts and firmly believes in something, it manifests in your life at once.

The human mind functions according to preconceived beliefs. It continues to manifest the same old experiences in your life as long as you don't impress it with new healthy thoughts. Hence, it is imperative that you prepare a fresh framework of healthy beliefs, which abounds in love, joy, perfect health and creativity. Repeatedly read and feel these new belief statements at least a hundred times every day until they get ingrained into your inner mind.

Repetition of new healthy beliefs is the secret to re-program the mind. When new beliefs are repeated passionately and frequently, they replace the old belief patterns. Make use of the re-programmability of the mind and DNA to attain perfect health. Put positive words to use by consciously and lovingly repeating them. Memorize these positive belief statements by heart so that they can be instilled into the inner mind.

You may repeat these belief statements by resting in a relaxed posture, either sitting on a chair or lying down on the bed. The potency of spoken words increases manifold when your body is relaxed. If possible, make a poem out of all your chosen belief statements. Sing the poem to yourself in a lulling tune. Melody and harmony are infallible catalysts for creating deep positive impressions on the mind.

Affirmation to erase mental scars

We need not feel beaten down or depressed if we are humiliated or abused. Childhood scars caused by rebuke and abuse leave a lasting impression on people, who then lead a constricted life. Such mental scars hamper the physical growth of the child, causing them to live a stunted life. The grown-up remains timid and afraid of owning up responsibilities. This leads to ailments of the shoulders and legs, since it's the shoulders that take up responsibility and legs that make us progress further.

If you have ever been subjected to intimidation or rebuke or abuse that has had a lasting impression on you, then you may repeat the following affirmation:

I have full faith in my divine plan.

Hence, I am now ready to progress further.

The Universe is blessing me with courage.

Hence, I can now take up new responsibilities.

Day by day, I am becoming more secure and healthy

Affirmations to heal illness

To heal any disease, repeat the following affirmation with love and faith:

I have understood the magic of the Laws of Health. My health is now becoming better and better.

I am becoming proficient in healing myself. All the problems of my life are rapidly dissolving.

Everything that is perfect and right for me is happening in my life as per my Divine plan.

In every minute, in every way, my body is getting better and better. I am a child of God. Hence, NO disease can harm me.

Besides abiding by the Laws of Health, also examine the real cause of disease. Is it due to improper diet, or irregular sleep habits, or due to inadequate exercise? If you have no such incorrect habits then ask yourself: "What are the inappropriate thoughts or feelings that I am entertaining in my mind, which are causing this ailment?"

When you are not able to find a tangible cause for the disease in your body, then the culprit has to be some inappropriate thoughts. Repeat the following affirmation to get rid of these inappropriate thoughts that hamper the healing process.

I now release my limiting beliefs.

I let go of the improper thoughts that have caused this disease. I am now free and healthy.

I am the source of happiness.

Repeat the above affirmations at least a hundred times over and then culminate them with a declaration of freedom from disease – *I am free; I am freedom.*

Visualize that you are being taken through the process of healing. Bring forth the feeling that you are experiencing the effect of healing.

Whenever you feel it necessary, repeat a selection of affirmations from the following –

- I am freed from negative thoughts and now abide in Peace.
- I have faith in divine providence; hence I am always happy and secure.

- I am at peace with myself; I am worthy of love and abundance.

- I am complete; I love, accept and forgive myself completely.

- I deserve to love and to be loved.

- I feel lively and fresh; I love to care for all the parts of my body. I am celebrating life.

- I believe that everything that is happening in my life is perfect and at the right time.

- I am consciousness; I joyously flow with every experience of life.

- Everything in my life is moving towards becoming better and better.

- I readily and happily let go of my past and am now comfortably stable in my present.

- Happy thoughts are giving rise to the state of complete health within me.

Record these powerful affirmations in your own voice on some recording device or on your mobile phone. Listen to these recorded affirmations at least once a day, in the morning, afternoon or at night in a relaxed disposition, being seated or lying down.

Besides this, you can also use the following method. Pick one or two such affirmations and write them down in your diary 10 to 20 times. Read them out aloud. If possible, give it a little tune and rhythm so that you can joyfully hum them. Through the day, whenever you remember those thoughts, let your heart and mind dwell in them. When you continuously focus your attention on such new beliefs, they manifest in your reality.

Check your Thoughts

When we are in the midst of testing circumstances, many of us tend to indulge in negative self-talk. Holding on to pessimistic thoughts and focusing on negativity can attract a host of problems in life. We tend to focus on illness by indulging in such self-talk –

- I don't know when this illness will go away.
- I hope this particular disease doesn't infect me.
- Will I be ever able to get rid of my obesity?
- I hope I don't suffer from heart disorders.
- The weather is very unpredictable these days; I hope I don't fall sick.
- Human life is so fragile that even a seemingly healthy person can fall sick.
- There are increasing incidences of viral infections these days.
- No matter how much I exercise, I tend to put on weight.
- I was drenched in the rain yesterday; I am bound to catch a cold and flu.

Nowadays, even young people are suffering from heart attacks.

These were some examples that you may have often heard people saying. When one harbours such self-defeating thoughts, it strengthens the feeling of fear within the body. This physically manifests as an imbalance in blood circulation. Over a period of time, symptoms become adverse and prominent all over the body. The person begins to feel lethargic and drained of energy.

The way out is to simply focus on your health. Root out all negative or pessimistic thoughts. Remain alert when any negative thought arises and immediately shift your focus to affirmations of healthy and wholesome living.

Here are some more health-infusing affirmations. You may choose to repeat the ones that resonate the most with you, frequently during the day with a deep feeling of conviction.

Perfect health is my birthright.

I am in favour of health; I am becoming healthier day by day.

I am brimming with life energy.

I am practicing physical exercise consistently.

My enthusiasm and health are getting better with every passing day.

I am in favour of health, not illness.

I have an efficient digestive system that can easily digest and assimilate food.

My fitness and freshness inspires others.

I am getting better and healthier with every passing breath.

My face is resplendent with the health and vitality that I am feeling within.

Divine energy is flowing through every cell in my body.

I am becoming aware about healthy living with every passing day.

My mind and body are powerful expressions of the Source.

I want to become healthy and fit; my body is changing for good.

My efficiency and stamina are rising with every passing day.

My body is becoming agile and healthy due to well-balanced diet, proper exercise and focused attention.

I am taking in the right amount of food at the right time.

My healthy body helps me express my highest potential.

I feel graceful and light.

Now slowly hum the prayer given below with the feeling of love and relaxed awareness.

I am God's creation.

Hence, the divine qualities of love, joy, and peace are permeating my heart and mind.

God has created nothing that can disrupt this divine harmony. The cause for disturbance within me is not in His divine order.

Just as a tired child finds respite in the mother's lap, I give in to Him and rest myself in His lap.

Waves of bliss are arising all around me. Being aware that I am within God, I am at peace. In His presence I am experiencing boundless Peace.

Thank you… Thank you… Thank you!

15

The Second Tool – GUIDED IMAGINATION

"Imagination is everything. It is the preview of life's coming attractions."

~ Albert Einstein

How true! Imagination is a boon provided to mankind. With the help of imagination, it is possible for us to acquire anything in life. But it can easily turn into a curse as well. This is because each of our thoughts is a prayer to nature, and nature doesn't play favourites. Whether the thoughts are positive or negative, nature fulfils them regardless.

The following experiment explains how the power of imagination works for health.

We will now guide our imagination and harness its power to make a part of the body more flexible and healthy. First read through the steps given below and then keep the book aside to perform it.

- Sit comfortably and close your eyes.

- Imagine how your body must have been as a child. Surely, it must have been sprightly and flexible. Today its condition may perhaps be different. Your reflexes, flexibility and wellbeing may have probably changed with age.

- Now through your imagination, see yourself as a little child again. With as much clarity as possible, see yourself running, hopping and skipping.

- Immerse yourself in the vivid moving scenes that you are imagining. Feel the energy and enthusiasm as much as you can.

- Remaining in those scenes, take a look at a chosen part of the body, which is painful or ailing today. See and feel how that part was working fine at that time. Even when you were jumping all over the place, that particular part was doing great.

- The key to this exercise is to deeply feel the same feelings that you used to feel as a child. Soak in the fresh air and the smell of wet soil as if you are actually playing outside.

Perform this simple but creative exercise regularly for a few days. If practiced effectively, it is highly possible that you will see a miraculous transformation in the troubled part of your body.

We have both rich and poor memories. Rich memories are happy recollections that reverberate positively in our body-mind mechanism. Poor memories are associated with negative emotions like regret, guilt, hatred, grief, that destructively interfere with the in-built healing intelligence.

The mind has the habit of raking up sorrowful incidents and indulging in directionless thoughts. This habit needs to be broken. We nurture poor memories by recalling and reliving them again and again. We should refrain from doing so. Perform the guided imagination exercise to give your thoughts a definite direction. This exercise makes use of rich memories that have the power to change our present.

Guided imagination can be used to good effect for attaining health. Let us understand how.

As we have already seen earlier, our bodies are in a state of constant flux. Old cells die and new ones take birth. No part of the body remains the same for more than a few years. Each and every cell of the body must die and give way to a new one. This means that diseases should not last long because the diseased cells will no longer exist. Yet, we see some people suffering forever. Why? Because old cells pass on their memories to new cells in the process of cell division. This is a groundbreaking revelation, which can be understood further with the help of an example.

When a school teacher trains his successor just before retiring, he tells him, "This particular student is mischievous; watch out for him. That child is impolite and careless. That third student cannot write properly..." As a result, the new teacher too nurtures the same perception towards his students. He inherits his predecessor's opinions and deals with the students accordingly. Since he starts behaving in the same way as the previous teacher, the students too continue to behave in the same manner. Thus the students never get a chance to improve themselves.

The retiring teacher ought to have taken care not to pass on any negative memory about any student to the new teacher. The new teacher too ought to have politely said to the retiring teacher, "Please don't tell me anything about the students; let me find out for myself. I don't want to have any preconceived notions about them. I wish to approach them with a fresh outlook."

If every teacher had such an outlook, the students would have improved and the teachers too would not have had to deal with troublesome students. It is often seen that troublesome students transform into courteous and diligent students when a likeable, caring teacher takes over. They behave very well with fresh-minded teachers who carry no mental baggage about their past.

You need to replicate this principle with your body. You need to remove memories of disease from your subconscious mind and program it for health. Since the subconscious mind controls every cell of the body, you may soon see your disease vanishing. Take advantage of the guided imagination technique to reprogram your subconscious mind with the radiant health you want.

Steps of the Guided Imagination Process

Guided imagination for health is a simple process comprising of six easy steps –

Step 1: Relax

The aim of this exercise is to actually feel the desired health while imagining it. If you are able to feel it, you will definitely gain it very soon. To feel it, your body and mind need to be relaxed and peaceful while doing this exercise. Take the following steps to relax your body and mind:

- Sit comfortably in a chair or lie down on your bed. Close your eyes.
- Count down slowly from 100 to 1 in your mind. This will help remove unwanted thoughts and enhance your concentration.
- Watch your breath while counting down. Inhale and exhale normally.
- Mentally suggest to each part of your body from the toes of your feet to the crown of your head, "Relax… relax… relax…" Give complete attention to each part of your body while instructing it to relax. With a peaceful mind, feel each part relaxing.
- By now your thoughts would have reduced and you would be feeling calm and relaxed. If you know of any other technique to relax your body and mind, you may use it.

Step 2: Visualize the scene of your goal

The most important thing in the guided imagination exercise is to visualize and believe that you have already achieved the thing you want. Feel happy that your longstanding wish has finally been granted to you. You must visualize the final picture and not the process of getting there.

For example, if your aim is to lose weight, you need to visualize the slim figure you will ultimately achieve. You need to imagine people telling you, "Wow! How did you become so fit? You are looking so energetic!" You must not visualize the process of exercising, working out in the gym, or following a diet chart. Don't tell yourself, "I will work out vigorously and follow a strict diet to reduce weight." Instead, tell yourself, "My body is feeling fresh, lively and light. Thank you for granting me fitness!"

Step 3: Visualize and feel only positive aspects

Next, visualize all the positive details of the final picture and don't forget to enjoy the feelings as well. Continuing the above example of weight loss, visualize that you have worn a smaller-sized T-shirt and jeans. Imagine yourself in front of the mirror, admiring yourself and feeling happy. You are enjoying the newfound feeling of lightness and agility. People around your are eagerly asking you for suggestions on health. Use positive and motivating words to express what you are feeling, like – exuberant, hale and hearty, peaceful, blissful, ecstatic.

Your subconscious mind does not understand negative words like 'no', 'I don't want', etc. For example if you say, "I don't want to be fat," your subconscious mind only registers the part about 'being fat' partand starts acting upon it! Hence, change your self-talk to "I have become slim and trim. My body weight is optimum." Feel the happiness, peace and enthusiasm. Then, your subconscious mind will initiate actions in your body and mind towards fulfilling the visualized goal. Your faculties will think only of the final picture.

Hence, take care not to affirm statements like: "I don't want this illness", "I hate diabetes", "God knows when this disease will go away". Instead, affirm to yourself, "I am now freed from this disease", "I am feeling wonderful after overcoming diabetes", "I am thrilled to become completely self-reliant" and so on. Instead of saying, "I wish I were as agile as before", say, "I am as agile and fit as ever."

Step 4: Pray to the Source

You can also pray for health during this exercise. Pray to the Source – the enlivening consciousness. Everything, including health, is created from the Source. When you pray to the Source for health, you will begin to receive action cues through various pure channels. You need to take these cues and act.

For example, you might meet a doctor who can guide you through the healing process. You might come across a book that provides easy solutions to your health issues. You might get acquainted with a physical trainer or therapist who understands the needs of your body and suggests suitable exercise.

Step 5: Put faith into action

Express your faith in the Source through your actions. If your goal is to lose weight so as to be fit, go and buy smaller-sized clothes in advance. With such faith in your heart, create and ingrain a happy image of the ideal result in your brain. Whenever negative thoughts start troubling you, recall this image and keep strengthening it through happy feelings. Every day, pray and look forward to the materialization of this image.

Step 6: Purify your mind to gain a healthy body

The final step is to keep in mind the following laws of nature:

- Celebrating others' health is like opening the gateway to your own health.
- If you wish to gain health, help others gain it.

You can use the power of guided imagination to help others as well. When you imagine for yourself, many negative thoughts can appear in your mind. You may feel apprehensive of the results. This is because we generally tend to be attached to our own problems. But when you perform the same imagination exercise for others, you do so with detachment. You don't get many negative thoughts when you are detached from others' problems. Hence, imagine that others are also enjoying the health that you aspire for.

If you want to get rid of a particular disease, you can pray for others who suffer the same disease. Very often, this approach can be even more effective than praying for yourself! Your subconscious mind gets programmed in the same manner, with the same mental images, but with the added benefit of cheerfulness resulting out of detachment.

Use of a Vision board to aid guided imagination

When you surround yourself with images of the physical health that you wish to experience, about the healthy habits that you wish to inculcate, it helps clarify and concentrate on what you have imagined. Visual depiction helps reinforce the picture of your goal in the mind's eye. You may go through magazines and cut out images that depict a healthy body, agility, strength, flexibility and healthy food. You can then paste these selected pictures on a vision board that you will always be in your sight.

Benefits of the Power of Guided Imagination

Guided imagination can be used not just to attain the pinnacle of health, but also for the following other benefits –

1. Improved concentration: Guided imagination can help you improve your ability to concentrate. This is an important key to achieve your goals in life. As soon as you start guiding your imagination towards a particular goal, your thoughts become intense and work like a magnet for attracting the goal. You can attract opportunities, people, skills and anything else that you need by using this technique.

Direct all your thoughts and feelings in one direction, towards the goal you aspire for. Focus all your energy on the goal, exactly as one focuses sun rays on one spot by passing them through a magnifying glass. You have seen the power of such focus – the sun rays can literally torch a stack of paper in no time. The power of imagination and concentration work in the same way.

2. Goal-oriented biochemical events in the body: When your mind visualizes a certain scene, whether real or imagined, corresponding biochemical events are triggered in the body, which help in dealing with the situation and getting to the destination. If you are in a scary situation or you imagine one, your body secretes adrenalin, your heart pumps faster, your muscles flex, and your pupils dilate. This helps the body in preparing for a fight-or-flight response to achieve safety.

Similarly if you see or imagine a delicious food item, your mouth salivates to help digesting it if you eat it. Thus, mere imagination is enough to set off biochemical events in the body. Take advantage of this power to achieve the health you want. See your health goals clearly in your imagination and you will receive corresponding help from your body.

3. Augments learning ability: An experiment was conducted at Harvard University. Two groups of students were assigned a particular task. The first group was asked to first visualize the task from start to end. The second group was asked to directly begin with the task. At the end of the allotted time, the first group had already completed the task exactly in the manner they had visualized. The second group had completed only 55% of the task.

Almost every accomplished athlete makes use of the power of guided imagination. Jack Nicklaus, regarded as the greatest golf player of all time has revealed, "*I never hit a shot, not even in practice, without having a very sharp, in-focus picture of it in my head. First I see the ball where I want it to finish. Then I see the ball going there; it's path, trajectory, shape and even its behaviour on landing. The next scene shows me making the kind of swing that will turn the previous images into reality.*"

You too can make use of guided imagination to learn something new in a more effective and time efficient way by shadowboxing through it.

4. Creative thoughts: The power of guided imagination hones creativity. Novel thoughts regarding whatever you imagine begin to appear in your mind. You may probably be flooded with creative thoughts when you wake up in the morning, when you shower, or when you drive to work. This is because you have set your vision only on the goal.

Many people tend to lose their ability to retrieve memory as they age. Such people can make use of the power of imagination to improve their memory retention and retrieval. If they fill their mind with visuals of those times when they were sharp and bright, their brain cells can become as active as before.

During the process of guided imagination, the subconscious mind cannot differentiate between a past scene, the present scene, or the future. It simply considers it as a present occurrence and brings about similar results. With the help of guided imagination you can regain lost suppleness, sharpness and enthusiasm.

Look at the part of your body, which is ailing today. Using the technique of guided imagination, recall how it was in the pink of health a few years ago. Visualize and feel its past health. This exercise will replace poor memories with rich ones.

Some questions for your contemplation:

1. Which rich memories can I recall to boost my health?

2. What is the purpose of my life? What direction should I lend to my imagination?

Action plan to practice guided imagination:

1. Clearly visualize the experience of health that you wish for.
2. Use guided imagination to replace poor memories with rich ones, so as to regain health.

16

The Third Tool – FAITH FAIR BOOK

In our daily lives, we are generally caught up with everyday activities in a way that most of us seldom find time to introspect and re-think our values, our principles and our goals. We also seldom find someone with whom we can share with an open heart about our deepest feelings and revelations, about our contemplation and intentions.

We make key decisions about how we intend to progress in various facets of life, about the kind of life we would love to lead. But the biggest problem is that all this remains a fantasy only in our minds. We do not find enough time to write about what we aspire for, about how we have decided to live each day, and why.

The result of this is stress, disharmony, frustration, health problems, and a general lack of clarity that reflects in everyday situations. We don't achieve anything productive when we keep vacillating in our heads about what we really need and why.

However, when we note down the details about what we plan to do, about what our deepest intentions are, and why we would like to live the way we wish to, we will begin to experience a newfound peace and clarity. Putting down our thoughts on paper helps us empty the unnecessary mental clutter and create space for new ideas and new possibilities to emerge.

The Faith Fair Book is a tool that helps you gain clarity about what you really want in life and why. It is like your personal companion, that will accompany you every day, every moment, reminding you about your life choices, your key decisions, the principles that you live by.

You can write details in the Faith Fair Book about how exactly you wish to lead your life. Each one of us has our own unique set of values and aspirations. When it comes to health, this uniqueness is clearly visible because each one's body has a unique constitution.

As explained earlier, our bodies can either be phlegm predominant (*Kapha Dosha*), bile predominant (*Pitta Dosha*) or air predominant (*Vaata Dosha*). The proportion of these bodily humours varies from person to person. Remedies applicable to one person may not be applicable to another.

Benefits of the Faith Fair Book for health

We shall now look at the benefits of the Faith Fair Book for health.

1. Clarity of the goal

Writing down your goal in precise detail increases the probability of getting there faster. We have seen from the first law that everything exists first in the mental plane as thoughts before it manifests in physical reality. When your thoughts are placed carefully on paper with full faith in the manifestation process of the Source, such writing serves as a critical tool to aid in the manifestation.

What you write down after contemplation goes deep within your mind. You lend your conscious attention to it. This also helps in arousing positive feelings about the goal. Conscious attention and enthusiasm are pivotal factors in realizing your goal, as we've seen in the second law.

Writing down your goals in precise detail is also the most effective way to gain clarity of what you truly want. Based on the third law, writing directs your attention to what you really want, by de-focusing from what you don't want.

Clearly knowing what you want, why you want, and when you want helps you to evaluate when you are on track, or when you stray off track from the life path that you wish to take.

- Contemplate upon the following questions and write down the revelations.
- What does health really mean for me?
- What do I exactly want?
- What is the clear demand that I should place with the Source?
- What are the cues regarding health that I have been receiving from the Source?

- What are the follies that I've committed that have pushed me off the road to health?

This tool need not be restricted to the pursuit of health alone; it can also be effectively used to realize whatever you wish for in the social, professional, financial and spiritual facets of your life.

2. Health benefits

The higher your health goal, the more you will need to maintain the Faith Fair Book. It helps maintain sharp focus on the goal without being influenced by negative circumstances like sickness that may occur on the path.

3. Positive programming

By writing the Faith Fair Book of health, your subconscious mind gets programmed positively. The Universe is convinced that you are indeed sincere and committed to what you really want. Writing down your goals helps you align your thoughts, feelings, words and actions, thereby making the seventh law work in your favour. It is one way of communicating to nature that you really wish for what you have written.

You get inspired about your goals when you write the Faith Fair Book. This is because your hands, eyes and brain concentrate simultaneously and harmoniously. As a result, the image of what you want is embedded deep within your inner mind, leading to positive results.

4. Clarity of action plan for health

The action plan for gaining health unfolds before your eyes by writing your health goals in the Faith Fair book. You gain clarity on what to eat and why, what not to eat and why, what exercise to perform and why, which habits to break and why, which habits to develop and why. Merely by giving precise words to your thoughts, you gain immense clarity regarding your action plan.

5. Time saving and development of qualities

When your goal is unclear or muddled, your thoughts tend to meander into unproductive channels, thereby dissipating your time and energy. When your goal is clearly laid out before you, you save time. Your energy starts flowing in your chosen direction. This also improves your confidence, because the Faith Fair Book imparts firmness to your thoughts and raises your willpower.

How to write the Faith Fair Book for Health

1. Use a single diary and follow a writing system

The first rule is to use a single diary for your Faith Fair Book of health. Also, follow a systematic method of writing to avoid irritation later on. Without a systematic method, you will forget where you noted something important and thereby waste time and efforts in finding or re-writing it. Instead of a diary, you may also use your computer, tablet or mobile phone for efficiently managing your notes.

2. Write only 'what you want'

As with the technique of guided imagination, while writing the Faith Fair Book, you must focus only on what you want, not on what you don't want. Don't write: 'I don't want illness.' Write: 'I want to enjoy the joy of health.' What you write in your Faith Fair Book will become your reality. Hence, use only wholesome, positive and inspirational words. Remember that positive words program your subconscious mind positively.

Here are a few examples:

Don't write: I don't want to fall sick.

Instead, write: I want to enjoy the joy of health.

Don't write: I don't want to be overweight.

Instead, write: I want to be healthy, fit and lively with optimum weight.

Don't write: I will need to take a lot of effort to become fit.

Instead, write: With proper diet, exercise, adequate rest and recreation, I can easily become fit.

In addition, you can write down the following affirmations for physical health:

- *I am healthy and agile. I am enjoying being fit and lively.*
- *I eat the right quantity of proper food at the right time.*
- *My healthy body is efficiently helping me to fulfil the ultimate goal of my life.*

- *I am feeling light and sprightly.*
- *I am a child of God. No disease can touch me.*

3. Write everything clearly and precisely

A motivational coach once asked his audience during a seminar, "How many of you want more money?"

Many participants raised their hands. The trainer handed out a ten-dollar bill to each one of them and asked, "You now have more money than before. Are you satisfied?"

They all smiled, "No, this won't suffice."

The trainer then handed out a hundred-dollar bill to each and asked, "Are you happy now?"

"No, we need a lot more!"

Even with health, people want 'more'. But most people don't have a clear idea of how much is 'more'. Write down in precise terms about the health that you want for yourself. Using the word 'more' in general baffles the subconscious mind. Ask yourself, "What do I exactly want?".

Don't write: I need to reduce my weight.

Instead, write: My weight shall be …… kg by ……[date].

Don't write: I want to exercise for a long time every day.

Instead, write: I exercise for …… minutes every day, beginning at …… o'clock.

Don't write: I want to get rid of diabetes.

Instead, write: My blood sugar shall reduce to and stabilize at ...... units by ...... [date] and I will enjoy permanent freedom from diabetes thereafter.

Don't write: I want to strengthen my muscles.

Instead, write: Within the next ...... months, my biceps and triceps will be so strong that I will be able to lift ...... kilograms for ...... time without tiring.

4. Append your goal statement with '*so that…*'

In your Faith Fair Book, you need to clearly state the reason why you want to achieve your health goals. This will make it easier for you to achieve them.

Here are a few examples:

- I want to gain complete health *so that* I can take giant strides towards success in my chosen field.
- I want to exercise regularly *so that* my immunity improves.
- I want divine energy to flow through my body *so that* I enjoy every moment of life.
- I want every cell of my body to be healthy *so that* I can face any challenge.
- I want to follow a proper diet, exercise and good lifestyle *so that* I become friends with health.
- I want my body to remain healthy and peaceful till the very end *so that* I enjoy the joy of abundance in every facet of life – social, mental, financial and spiritual.

- I want to become healthier and wealthier with every passing day *so that* I enjoy physical vitality and financial prosperity in life.

- I want every part of my body to brim with energy and enthusiasm *so that* I'm able to give my hundred percent to any task.

- I want to achieve complete development in the physical plane *so that* my body can freely express the divine qualities of the Source.

- I want to adopt healthy practices *so that* I can attain the wealth of health.

5. Write with Faith

We can create anything that we wish in our lives. The Source has lent this power to human expression, but most people are unaware of this.

We are born with incredible power. We have just forgotten how to use it. Hence, the need is to awaken the power of faith. The Faith Fair Book will help awaken it. The only requirement is to keep faith! If you write the diary for your health in full unquestioning faith, you are bound to experience a miraculous transformation in your health. So, realize your faith and surrender completely to the Source while writing your Faith Fair Book.

6. Read with Faith

Mere writing is not enough, unless what you have written is reinforced through consistent reading.

Read the list of your goals three to four times a week, and activate your creative powers. Spend some time reflecting on the list. Go through it in full faith with a feeling of fulfilment. Close your eyes and imagine each goal as if you have achieved it. Take a pause to feel what it is like to have achieved the goal. Stay in this feeling of fulfilment for some time.

This experiment will activate your willpower. It bridges the gap between the present state of health and the imagined state. By continuously reinforcing the belief that you have already achieved your goal, you are only helping the Source manifest it in your life.

Don't forget to read your health diary at least three to four times a week, either upon waking up in the morning or before going to sleep at night. If you are travelling, you can write your goals and affirmations on little cue cards that can be kept handy in your pocket. You can make use of modern gadgets as well. You can create screen savers or mobile alerts for health reminders so that your focus never wanders away from health.

17

The Fourth Tool – FORGIVENESS

Suppose you are visiting a strange banquet. Strange, because the various stalls at the banquet offer not food, but thoughts. The rule of this strange banquet is that you can visit only one stall and pick only one thought of your choice.

The first stall offers a hot and spicy dish called 'anger'. The second stall offers a bitter dish called 'hatred'. The third one offers a pungent dish called 'worry'. The fourth offers a sweet dish called 'pleasure', while the fifth stall offers a bland dish called 'boredom'. Many such stalls follow.

The last one offers a wholesome dish called 'forgiveness'. The stall of forgiveness is somewhat deserted compared to the teeming crowd at the other stalls.

Most people in the party seem to be in some kind of pain or illness. But only a few people appear fresh, light and healthy. These are the ones present at the forgiveness stall. When these few people are asked the secret of their wellbeing, they say, "The only secret of our wellbeing is forgiveness. Forgiveness has freed us from every pain, sickness and irritation."

Indeed, every person visiting the forgiveness stall returned with the wealth of love, joy, peace, abundance and complete health.

The banquet in the above analogy symbolizes life on Earth. The various stalls represent the thoughts that the mind wishes to chew on again and again. The names of the dishes represent the emotions that arise when we chew on these thoughts. The food that we keep chewing on has a radical effect on our health, either positive or negative.

How would you like to return from the banquet? If you wish to return with cheer and lightness, you need the wholesome intake of forgiveness.

If one says, "Why should I take this medicine? I am not sick," it only means that they need a greater dosage of this medicine. Most people on Earth think that they don't need to forgive or seek forgiveness. A common reaction is, "Why should I apologize or ask for forgiveness when I haven't done any wrong?" This very reaction reveals that they haven't grasped the depth of forgiveness.

Forgiveness is the panacea that uproots every vice and illness, provides us physical, mental and social health, and puts us at ease and contentment. It works like a broom to clean out the toxins of resentment, pain, guilt and hatred. It applies a soothing balm to heal the deepest of wounds in the inner mind.

With the fourth law of health, we have seen that we receive evidences in our everyday life for whatever we believe about the world. The more evidences we receive, the more our beliefs get reinforced.

Many of us tend to make wrong assumptions or judgments about our family, friends or colleagues due to some apparently negative incidents. We have seen that the grudges we hold within, causes emotions to reside as impressions in our cellular memory. These impressions are seeds of disease. They mature, proliferate and then appear as visible symptoms.

We can invite health into our lives only when our minds are cleansed off these impressions. We need to get rid of these poor memories. Our mistaken assumptions and judgments have led to undesirable reactions from us – negative words that we have spoken in the past, negative thoughts and feelings of hatred, anger, guilt, fear, boredom and depression. All this negativity continues to reside in our bodies as poor cell memories even today. These poor memories drain energy from the cells of the body, making us dull and weak.

Seeking forgiveness from the parts of your body

Let us take a look at some common health disorders and understand the play of negative thoughts behind them. The common treatment for all such illnesses is forgiveness. When you seek forgiveness from the parts of your body, they receive the power to heal themselves.

1. Eye and eyesight disorders

When you feel like turning a blind eye to certain situations or people due to hatred or fear, it can precipitate as disorder of the eyes or eyesight.

You may not wish to even see those people who may have insulted or abused you physically or mentally. You may have seen gruesome incidents like fatal traffic accidents or extreme poverty. Such incidents can possibly trigger a constant self-talk, "I don't want to see this person's face again", "I don't want to see poverty or disease again" etc. Such negative self-talk sends signals to your cellular memory that you don't want to *see* things clearly. This can potentially manifest as blurring of vision, visual impairment, swelling or irritation in the eyes.

'Eye drops' of forgiveness: Forgiveness serves as therapeutic drops that can restore health to your eyes! Seek forgiveness, in your mind if not directly, from those for whom you may have harboured feelings of hatred or fear. Also forgive everyone for the hurtful feelings they may have caused you.

If you get thoughts like, "I can never forgive this person," it is helpful to remember that not forgiving them is like punishing yourself for what apparently they may have done. It is in your own interest that you forgive them so that you can enjoy the beauty of life.

Also seek forgiveness from your eyes for having suppressed its vision by refusing to see the depth and variety of the world. Forgiveness can help in healing your eyesight so that you can again behold all the colours of life in their full glory.

2. Headache

One of the most probable causes of headache, including migraine, is pent-up anger and bitterness. It has been researched and observed that illnesses such as headache, migraine, heartburn (acidity) and sinusitis can be psychosomatic in nature, their primary cause being anger. One of the most effective ways to achieve freedom from pent-up anger is forgiveness.

The balm of forgiveness: To get rid of anger and its associated illness, it is worth performing an experiment. Take time out and sit in a peaceful setting. List the names of all those due to whom you feel angry – the list may perhaps include your employer, business associates, spouse, children, close relatives, and so on. Also include those people who may have caused you anger in the past, either dead or alive. Mentally bring each one before your eyes. No matter how rude or wrong they may have appeared in the past, forgive them.

If you really love yourself, it helps to remember that you are only doing a favour on yourself by forgiving everyone wholeheartedly. Also seek forgiveness from everyone. If needed, personally seek forgiveness from certain people, especially family members. No matter who was at fault, tell yourself: "I apologize because I love myself. I reacted with anger in a situation that was actually giving me an opportunity to learn and grow."

Also seek forgiveness from your liver and lymphatic system for the trouble caused by suppressed anger. The balm of forgiveness can soothe and heal the root cause of headache.

3. Throat-related illnesses

The throat is known to be the seat of human expression. If you frequently suffer from throat-related illnesses like cough and cold, sore throat, swelling, tonsillitis or thyroid dysfunction, drink the syrup of forgiveness!

The syrup of forgiveness: Common cold is known to be a result of confusion or choke-up in the flow of thoughts. Swelling of the throat can be traced to suppression of negative feelings arising from inability to speak up. Similarly, unfulfilled and suppressed desires can potentially manifest in the form of thyroid and tonsillitis.

The remedy for throat-related problems is the syrup of forgiveness! Seek forgiveness from the throat for all those instances when you have choked or suppressed expression under the influence of fear, guilt or sorrow. Forgiveness will clear the path for your expression.

4. Backache

The back and shoulders are symbols of support. One of the major functions of the back and shoulders is to support body weight and maintain postural balance during activities. The cause of backache and shoulder pain is burden. When financial, emotional or social responsibilities seem like burden, which seems too heavy to bear, it shows up as pain in the back and shoulders.

The painkiller of forgiveness: Identify the cause of your mental, emotional or financial burden and practice forgiveness for it. This is the most effective painkiller to get rid of back pain! You may probably have not taken care of your posture. Whatever be the reason, lovingly invite your back into your field of attention and seek its forgiveness.

Seek forgiveness from the Source for ignoring its presence in your life and taking all the burden of life upon yourself. Henceforth, remember to fallback on the Source during difficult times. When you rest in the presence of the Source, your burdens are released.

5. Heart-related ailments

The heart is a symbol of love, faith and joy. It is noteworthy that people suffering from recurring heart disease often tend to be subject to bouts of depression and suppression. Very often, the cause for depression is lack of love. When we experience true love, our heart warms to it and opens out to embrace life. However, when we lack the experience of true love, being stifled by testing situations, we tend to close our heart and experience negative emotions like hatred, bitterness, envy, and guilt. These emotions manifest as blockages in the circulatory system, leading to a host of heart diseases.

The potion of forgiveness: Drink the potion of forgiveness every day to be free from heart disease! When your heart fills with the nectar of forgiveness, neither will you crave for love nor will you feel like holding onto grudges for anyone. Forgiveness opens us to the experience of true love.

Also seek forgiveness from your body for not giving it timely and adequate exercise, proper diet and sleep. This goes a long way in improving the health of our physical heart and circulatory system.

6. Digestive disorders

When you are not able to digest certain experiences in life due to fear or hatred, they manifest as digestive disorders. Bloating, belching, indigestion and constipation are invariably the result of holding onto fear or hatred towards someone or something. If you don't wish to let go of bitter experiences or forgive certain people, then such resentment can restrain the digestive system and cause disorders.

The pills of forgiveness: The unnecessary thoughts and feelings that we nurture for years manifest as gastro-intestinal disorders. The pills of forgiveness can soothe and heal such disorders of the gut! Seek forgiveness every morning and night from your intestines by saying, "*I unnecessarily made you store the refuse of fear, hatred and anxiety. I am sorry. Please forgive me.*"

7. Greying or loss of hair

When we lose our sense of focus in chaotic and directionless thoughts, blood supply to the hair reduces. Thoughts that cause stress, anxiety or hatred create stiffness in the muscles of the neck and shoulders, and impair blood circulation to the head, causing greying or loss of hair. Most people in today's fast-paced world are grappling with premature thinning or greying of hair.

The conditioner of forgiveness: For healthy hair, apply the conditioner of forgiveness! Once you feel relaxed and peaceful, run your hands lovingly through your hair and say, "*Please forgive me. I obstructed your source of nourishment due to my improper way of thinking. I created stress for you by persisting with anxiety and hatred. Please forgive me. Henceforth, I will be aware and apply the shampoo of love. I am sorry for having neglected you for so many years.*"

You may practice forgiveness every night by bringing the A-body of the concerned body-part into your field of awareness. This has brought about health miracles in the lives of hundreds of subjects. Consistent practice with faith and conviction can surely lead to healing and the attainment of a healthy natural state.

18

The Fifth Tool – GRATITUDE

The body is a marvellous creation – the most sophisticated machine on Earth. Have you ever wondered at the amazing intricacies of this machine? It is time we contemplated upon this gift so that we can utilize it in the most appropriate manner to achieve our life purpose. of life.

Your body is made of trillions of cells, all working in unison and harmony with each other. Countless processes are going on simultaneously throughout your body, even as you are reading this book right now. Your eyes are constantly relaying visual information to your brain. Various parts of your brain are active, processing the information you are reading. At the same time, your digestive system is busy processing the food you ate. Your respiratory system is working relentlessly to provide pure oxygen to your heart. Your heart is pumping at least seventy times a minute to provide enriched blood to all parts of the body. Your ears are listening to sounds and your nose is sensing the quality of air around you. Your skin is sensing the environment and responding to touch.

When you eat, your tongue acts as a monitor to check the food's edibility and nutritional value. Your pancreas produce suitable enzymes that assist the digestion of food. The heart labours to distribute blood suitably. The intestines work as a supplier of nutrients extracted from food. The skin works as a temperature regulator by producing the necessary amount of perspiration. Our body is a perfectly organized institution in itself.

Trillions of cells of our body are active at any given time! Not only are they active but they also interact with each other symbiotically. Each cell of the body has a communication centre, a power-house and a transportation system in addition to its functional systems. Countless processes go on in the body until its death. No part of the body interferes with the functioning of other parts. Yet, they all work in unison towards a common goal, a harmonious orchestra playing the symphony of life. If some part falls sick, the in built healing intelligence sets in through the immune system.

Medical science is advancing at such a rapid rate that we get to know more and more about the human body all the time. Yet, countless more secrets are yet to be revealed. The key question is: Do we ever take time to appreciate the most amazing machine on earth? Have we ever expressed our gratitude to our bodies for working so magnificently for us? We engage in various activities from morning to night with enthusiasm and liveliness only due to the unconditional support of our bodies.

Our body co-operates with us ceaselessly and untiringly. We ought to take note of this and express our sincere gratitude to each of its parts and organs. Gratitude is the password to complete health!

Experiencing and expressing gratitude for whatever you have received in life can be a miraculous experience. It fills your life with peace and serenity. Accept everything with a deep sense of gratitude, be it nature, the people around you. Be primarily grateful to your body that serves as a medium for your experience of life and your expression.

The Source expresses itself as harmony, peace, love, joy and abundance through our bodies. When we thank the Source for bringing forth perfect health as per our divine plan, we are seeing health as already given. This is the most powerful way of attaining perfect health from the Source.

Gratitude helps you to be in a state of harmony with your divine plan. It makes you receptive to the unfolding of your highest possibility for health. Gratitude removes fear and worry that come with the limiting belief of lack of health.

If you remain focused only on the illusion of disease and disability, you entangle and constrict the same universal powers and plant the seeds of disease. It helps you to see the hidden truth of perfect health of the Source instead of getting entangled in the illusion of illness.

When you say "Thank You for health," you send a signal to the Universe that you see only the truth of perfect health. Then the Universe rallies behind you and the healing intelligence of the Source begins to work through your body.

Even if you have fallen sick, identify it as an illusion. Good health is waiting at your doorstep; it wants to come in and provide healing. But when you refuse to see it, how can it come in? The illusion of sickness blocks its entry into your life. Gratitude is the way of seeing through the clouds of illness and welcoming the sunlight of health.

Thank your body for serving you and apologize for misusing it. Many people tend to blame their bodies for not living up to their expectations. They keep finding flaws with their bodies and comparing it with others. In doing so, they invite disease.

Accept your body as it is and express gratitude for it. Praise your body for its existence.

Every day, take some time from your routine and look at your body from a new perspective. Close your eyes and lovingly caress your face, head and shoulders with your palms. Thank them for working so well all these years and encourage them to keep working well hereafter.

A classical instrumentalist tunes his strings before a musical performance. With eyes closed, he immerses himself completely in tuning each string to precision. In the same way, we need to precisely tune our body with the Source.

Let us thank each part of our body, starting from the head, slowly leading to the feet.

Brain

The brain is the control centre of our body. Through a highly intricate system of nerves, it sends signals to every corner of the body and supervises its processes. Not only this, but it is also because of the brain that our thoughts can be translated to the physical realm. It is the brain that enables cognition of the senses. Thank this vital centre of your body. Also seek forgiveness for polluting it with negative thoughts and feelings.

Eyes

Eyes are the means with which you witness the world, enjoy beautiful scenes, read and gain an understanding of the world. But you may perhaps be causing strain to your eyes by exerting them without giving them adequate rest. Thank the eyes for unconditionally supporting you. Apologize and seek forgiveness if they have been exerted without sufficient relaxation.

Ears

Ears play the crucial role of delivering sounds to us. Thank them for the joy they have given you all along. Thank them for the words of wisdom that enter your system. Seek their forgiveness for any inappropriate or negative inputs that they have been made to receive. Promise your ears that you will allow only the truth to be input through them.

Nose

The nose is a crucial input device. It senses the quality of air around you through smell and temperature; it filters dust and inhales safe air to keep the body alive. Seek forgiveness from the nose if you have subjected it to difficulties and encourage it to work better by helping it with breathing exercise.

Tongue

The tongue is a vital organ that produces words and gives verbal expression to your thoughts and feelings. It also doubles up as a food checker and provides you the pleasure of taste. Admire and appreciate the work of the tongue and thank it for all that it has facilitated for you. Many a times, we misuse the tongue for speaking ill, spreading negativity, and overindulging in sensory pleasure through unhealthy food. Wholeheartedly seek forgiveness from the tongue for such misuse.

Teeth

Without teeth you wouldn't be able to chew food. Thank them with love and assure them that you will keep them clean, healthy and strong.

Throat

The throat delivers food to the stomach. Vocal cords in the throat produce the voice with which we communicate and express ourselves. Thank your throat and assure it of your loving care.

Neck

The neck keeps your head connected to the rest of your body. Very often, we tend to neglect our neck and keep it in a wrong posture when we're engrossed with work. This can lead to conditions like spondylitis in the longer term. We shouldn't take the neck's flexibility and tenacity for granted. Seek forgiveness from the neck for its over-exertion and thank it for co-operating with you so far. Also promise to give it adequate exercise and relaxation.

Shoulders

All the responsibilities that you have taken in life so far have been borne by your shoulders. Appreciate and thank your shoulders with respect. Apologize if you have overburdened them on occasions with fear, stress and guilt.

Arms, wrists and hands

Seek forgiveness from your arms and hands for taking them for granted and using them carelessly. Thank them for their indispensable help in life and assure them that you will always take care of them.

Heart

The heart is one of the most important organs of the body. Without a moment's rest, it has been relentlessly pumping purified blood to each cell of the body since the birth of your body. Lovingly place your hand over your heart and thank it for its ceaseless contribution to life.

The area around the heart is also the place where the Source connects with the body. Express your gratitude to this gateway to the Source.

Seek forgiveness from the heart if you feel that you've burdened it with an unhealthy lifestyle or indulgence in negative emotions.

Back

The back, consisting of the vertebral column, supports and balances the whole body. It is due to the back that we can sit comfortably for hours. Express your gratitude for its enormous support. We don't always give enough respect to our back; we slouch, we slump, we sway. Apologize for making it undergo undue stress and strain and promise to maintain proper posture henceforth.

Lungs and respiratory system

Like the heart, the lungs too have been ceaselessly drawing in oxygen from the air you breathe and providing it to the body since the birth of your body. Whenever we encounter any kind of physical or mental stress, the lungs alter their pace of breathing to alert you to the stress, so that you can take appropriate action. Take a deep breath and thank your lungs and the entire respiratory system for the vital role they play. Seek forgiveness for not thanking them earlier and in case they have been abused by smoking.

Digestive system

The digestive system is the assimilator and distributor of nutrients to the body. It is a crucial contributor to our health and wellbeing. It digests the hardest of food items that we feed it. Express your gratitude to the digestive tract for keeping you active and digesting everything that your tongue craved for. Apologize and seek forgiveness for eating at untimely hours or burdening it with junk food. Give it the assurance that you will be alert about what food to eat and what food to avoid.

Hips

Hips are located at the centre of the body. It is from here that your body bends back and forth and sideways. Thank your hips for the flexibility and support they provide. With folded hands, seek forgiveness for troubling them by sitting in a wrong posture.

Reproductive system

Thank your reproductive system for creating a marvel in the form of your offspring and continuing nature's play on earth. Seek forgiveness from the system if it has been abused through indiscriminate indulgence.

Genes

Seek forgiveness from your genes if you have blamed them for the flaws that you percieve in your personality. Accept your genes the way they are and don't condemn them for the coming generations by programming them negatively.

Liver

The liver is responsible for digestion and purification of blood. It removes toxins from blood, thereby playing a very crucial role in keeping the body alive. Thank the liver for serving such a vital function relentlessly. Seek forgiveness from the liver if it has been abused through indulgence in unhealthy junk food or alcohol.

Urinary system

The urinary system comprising the kidneys, urinary bladder and urethra performs the important task of expelling liquid waste from the body and keeping it clean and healthy. Thank it for its vital role and promise to take care of it by drinking adequate water and avoiding harmful intake.

Legs

Legs are our vital means of mobility. We make use of this vehicle, but do we also maintain and service it? Seek forgiveness from your legs for not giving them adequate exercise and relaxation. Thank them for serving you so efficiently for so long.

Knees, elbows and other joints

Knees, elbows and other joints provide your body with flexibility. You are able to perform such a variety of actions and chores because of your joints. Thank them for providing you the opportunity to express yourself through physical action. Apologize for putting extra burden on them and assure them that you will take care of them hereafter. Incorporate essential nutrients in your diet to help strengthen your joints.

Bones and skeletal structure

The skeletal structure is the basic frame on which the body is built. Thank it for its foundational support. Take efforts to strengthen it with proper nutrition and exercise.

Muscles

Muscles give our body strength. Hence it is important to maintain a healthy and optimum muscle mass. Thank them for the strength and balance that they provide. Seek their forgiveness if they have not been toned and exercised.

Skin

The skin is the protective sheath of the body. Thank it for its immense service of protecting the body from atmospheric rigours. The skin is also a reflection of our health. The better our health, the more radiant our skin is. The complexion of skin does not matter; it does its job irrespective of complexion. Pray that your face and body always radiate great health. Seek forgiveness from the skin if it has been blamed for its complexion.

Vital force

The vital force flows throughout the body and enlivens all body parts. Take notice of it and give it special thanks.

Now thank and seek forgiveness from all other parts of the body that have not been addressed in this list. We have connected with each part very briefly in the above exercise. If you are suffering from any particular disease, disorder or disability, connect and deeply converse with the concerned body parts. Express your gratitude and repentance.

'Thank you' is not merely words; it is a feeling, a state. The power of this feeling will take you from ignorance to knowledge, from darkness to light, from blind faith to bright faith, from inner struggle to ultimate peace, from failure to success, and from illness to health. So, raise your arms out and express with deep feeling: "*Thanks for health… Thanks for health… Thanks for health…!*"

By doing this you connect with the Source. Whenever you go out for a jog in the park, observe every living or non-living thing you come across, like the rising sun, the vast sky, chirping birds, plants and trees, flowers, dew drops, the breeze. Be grateful for nature's grace.

Raise your arms and express your gratitude:

I am part of nature's infinitude.

I am tuned with the Source.

The rays of the sun are making my body and mind pure and healthy. Thanks to the Source for providing everything in abundance!

I am brimming with perfect health.

There is plenty of sunlight, clean air and clean water in this world. There is plenty of natural and wholesome food.

I am exercising regularly and improving my fitness. I am filled with enthusiasm.

I am blessed with healing and the right medication to get rid of all illness.

I am intuitively receptive to indications from nature for improving my health.

Thank you for bringing perfect health in my life…!

19

The Sixth Tool – ACCEPTANCE

This happened when Sir Isaac Newton was a professor at London's Trinity College, at the pinnacle of his career. One day, he was working in his room at night. Papers containing years of rigorous research were kept at his desk, illuminated by a candle. His pet dog Diamond was also in the room. Hearing a knock on the front door, Newton left the room leaving Diamond alone.

When he returned, Newton was aghast to see that the playful Diamond had toppled the candle and set all his papers on fire. Despite the incredible loss of years of hard work, Newton was surprisingly calm and considerate. He merely exclaimed, "Oh Diamond, little do you know the mischief you have done!"

Most people, in a similar situation, would have seethed with anger. Newton neither got angry nor admonished his dog. He simply dug into his work and started afresh with new zeal and passion.

This incident tells us about the power of acceptance. Newton could awaken positive energy to start his work all over again only because he patiently accepted the situation. This is the magic of acceptance. Let us now explore how the power of acceptance can help us attain perfect health.

If only I were slim… If only I didn't suffer this disease… If only my parents had brought me up well… If only I had fair complexion… If only I didn't have protruding teeth… If only I was taller… If only my nose was straighter… If only I could digest food easily… If only I had rich black hair…

This list of '*If only…*' can go on endlessly. People desperately hold on to dreams about how they would like their physical appearance to be. They are not able to accept the present state of their bodies. They constantly resist something. Some people forever curse the genetic disorders handed to them through heredity. When people remain stuck in negative self-talk, their health worsens further.

We have seen how the mind has a deep impact on the body. Despite knowing this, most of us find it difficult to keep ourselves fully healthy. Why? The key reason is non-acceptance. The body is a phenomenal orchestra, consisting of many systems playing simultaneously in perfect harmony. Due to various reasons, it is possible that one or more parts of the body may develop disorders or pain. When we don't accept this and constantly try to wish it away with irritation or anger, we distance ourselves from health.

Now please keep this book aside for a while and reflect. Which aspects of your health or your appearance are not acceptable to you? Which part of your body do you complain about? For example it could be obesity, height, complexion, dark circles under the eyes, greying hair, wrinkles on the skin, weakness of the body, indigestion, or something else.

Remember that it is very important to be honest while contemplating. Honest contemplation will reveal the body part or aspect of health that you resist.

Non-acceptance leads to illness

Non-acceptance of any part of the body or aspect of the body physiology can lead to disease. This is because by doing so, you place blocks in the flow of vital energy. The feeling of acceptance carries positive vibrations. As soon as we accept, our negative thoughts and feelings disappear and our vital energy resumes smooth flow to each cell of the body. This is exactly like how water resumes its full flow through a pipeline when clogs are removed. When you accept, your attention shifts from 'what is wrong' to 'what can be done to rectify it'.

Suppose you are overweight. If you are upset or feel disappointed when you look at yourself in the mirror, it means the feeling of non-acceptance is strong. Look in the mirror and ask yourself, *"Can I accept the fact that I am overweight?"* You may perhaps instantly say "No". But even then, ask yourself once again, "Can I accept the fact that *right now* I am overweight?" Most probably you may be prepared to accept it, because it sparks the hope of a turnaround.

As soon as you accept, your mind becomes peaceful and clear about what lies ahead. The crowd of thoughts that were muddling your awareness disappears, allowing you to think creatively of what steps you need to take. You start seeing solutions that you couldn't see before. You become capable of taking new decisions to improve your health.

Thus, acceptance doesn't mean remaining in the same condition and resigning to your negative feelings or 'fate'. It is totally the opposite. Once you accept the situation, the energy that was being wasted on negative feelings like disappointment, anxiety, fear, anger, or irritation becomes available to you for taking positive actions. You can make full use of this energy to passionately overcome your problems. In this way, acceptance makes you a problem-solver and not a failure like many people may believe.

Have you ever wondered why the fingers of your hand are dissimilar in size, strength and capability? Perhaps this never aroused your curiosity. You may have simply accepted them the way they were given to you. In this way you peacefully continued using them.

Each finger has its own unique role. This is not its weakness, but rather its beauty. When all the five fingers collectively work for the hand, it actually makes things easier. Together, the fingers of the hand can create divine music from instruments, bringing joy to everyone. This wouldn't have been possible if all fingers were identical. Similarly, each part of the body has its own speciality and role. You can watch this beautiful orchestra only when you are on the highest platform of acceptance.

It is possible to accept any of your health issues as easily as you have accepted your fingers. Some parts of your body are healthy, while some are not. See this variation through the eyes of acceptance. As soon as you accept it, it will initiate rejuvenation within your body.

Acceptance may initially seem like a trivial matter, but its importance and efficacy can be understood only after experiencing it for yourself. Mere acceptance can bring about a vast rise in your level of consciousness. Then your mind will find it easier to accept things even in adverse situations. Can you imagine what this process will ultimately lead you to? Perfect health!

Most people live under the impression that if they resist something, they will remain unaffected by it. But little do they realize that by opposing something, they are giving more attention to it. Consequently, they gravitate more and more towards the thing they don't want.

When you resist illness, your ability to overcome the illness reduces. Imagine trying to tie a shoelace with one hand, while the other hand is tied to your back. This is exactly what happens when you resist a situation. On the contrary, when you accept the situation, it is like freeing both your hands. You get a fresh surge of energy to tackle the problem. Whatever stress you have, vanishes.

When you accept the situation, the problem doesn't appear the same anymore because you view new dimensions and new solutions. This is because your subconscious mind starts seeking direct and straightforward solutions instead of dwelling on the problem. When you resist the problem, you tie yourself down and prevent yourself from working towards the solution.

Solutions can be found only from the state of acceptance. All great scientists and inventors have made use of this technique knowingly or unknowingly. When they couldn't find solutions to a problem, they would accept it and keep it aside for some time. Then suddenly, when their mind was completely calm and relaxed, they would hit upon their Eureka moments. You get answers from the Source when you least expect them.

Accept change

When people notice undesirable changes in their health, they begin to worry, "What has happened to me? All my life I was in the pink of health, and now I have fallen sick merely due to a change in weather…" They remain worried because they haven't accepted the fact. They blame other people or circumstances for their sickness. This gives them a false sense of solace.

If they accept changes in the state of their health, they can be at ease, making it possible for them to freely tackle the situation. Acceptance keeps us free from mental or emotional burden. It is only in such a relaxed state that can we can think creative ideas and solutions.

Suppose someone finds out during a routine check that he is diabetic. This news shakes him up and he remains depressed for a long time because he hasn't accepted this change. He may keep thinking, "I am just forty years old… now what will happen to me? Will I never get to enjoy sweets again? Does this mean that I will need to consume diabetic pills and take insulin shots throughout my lifetime?"

Such negative thoughts can easily spiral out of control. The first thought during any undesirable incident should be: "Can I accept this?" The mind may say, "No. I cannot." Allow some time to pass by and then again ask yourself, "Can I now accept this?" If your mind is still adamant on not accepting, ask yourself, "Okay. Then can I accept this non-acceptance at the least?" Even if you manage to accept that you are not able to accept the situation, it can ease the burden. This is the power of acceptance.

Make use of this power and accept every little change happening in your body. This will ensure that even the biggest of your fears have no ground to stand upon. Just like new leaves spring up with fresh abandon after autumn, consider change to be a source of joy, no matter how small or big it is.

20

The Seventh Tool – RELEASING

In the journey of life, man goes through various situations: he indulges in vices; he faces difficulties; he endures various diseases. However, it never occurs to him that the difficulty, the disease, is actually his unintentional need, an unknown wish that he has nurtured.

Many will find it difficult to believe that they face difficulties or illness because unknown to them, there is something within them that clings onto the illness or situation. It is hard to believe that a part of our own minds is working against us. However, this does happen, unknowingly, because of an hidden benefit, actually leading to self-sabotage.

At times, we experience that an illness persists for a long period and no known remedy seems to work. We might have tried all possible remedies and therapies to no avail. Also, there may be no visible reason for the occurrence of the illness or disorder. In most probability, the illness could be caused by our own hidden need to remain ill. We never want illness consciously. But a hidden need may exist within us, unknown to us, which continues to cling onto the illness. When we release this hidden need, the illness begins to miraculously dissolve!

Though the child has now grown up, there could still be some childhood notions, some hidden needs that you may have felt as a child, due to which you experience a sense of safety by clinging to a particular illness. This illusory sense of security manifests as a hidden need to cling to problems, to hold on to illnesses.

We will now look at some examples that will help clarify how this works within us.

Anita is fed up with her obesity. She weighs 85 kg. She has tried her best to lose weight. She has joined a weight-loss program at the gym, where she does weight training and aerobics on alternate days. She has consulted a dietician and follows weight-loss and detox diet. She consults her physical trainer to improve her workout. Despite all effort for six months, she is unable to lose much weight. The weighing scale still shows 84 kg.

When she is told that she may probably have a hidden need to remain obese, she rejects this idea initially. But when she agrees to look within and reflect deeply, she finds that obesity helps her in appearing less attractive. This is a learned way that her subconscious mind has adopted to avoid marriage, which her parents are insisting with her. Since childhood, she has observed the difficult circumstances that her mother has had to put up with to continue the marriage and bring up the children.

Obesity becomes a hidden need to avoid the responsibility of married life. Thus, remaining obese is Anita's way of escaping responsibility. It is also her way of feeling secure without being noticed as an eligible bachelor.

We can see from Anita's story that obesity and the lard of fat that accumulates around the abdomen can serve as hidden armour to escape responsibilities and activity. Many people are obese due to the deep need for avoiding attention from people around them. Though they may consciously try their best to lose weight, this hidden need at the subconscious level overrides all their effort. Given this knowledge, if they wish to lose weight, they will have to release this hidden need.

Jay is a spiritual seeker. He keeps attending various schools of spirituality and mediation. However, he is not doing well financially. He earns a fairly good salary, but is unable to see how he can be financially independent, so as to pursue his spiritual goal. He consults personal finance advisors and diligently invests in various financial instruments. Yet, after ten years, he finds that he is still far from being financially independent.

When he is made to contemplate upon his childhood beliefs and question his ideas about money, he is shocked to discover a deeply hidden need to avoid money! It turns out that during childhood, he has heard in spiritual congregations that people who are spiritually-minded pay no attention to money. His subconscious mind has been ingrained with a hugely self-defeating myth that money and spirituality cannot go together. This deep belief stops him from being wealthy!

If we have any such limiting beliefs, we should release them, as they do not serve our best endeavors to attain complete health. The truth is that complete health can be attained only when we make balanced progress in all facets of our lives viz. physical health, social harmony, financial abundance, mental maturity and spiritual growth.

There are many people who frequently fall ill with the slightest change in the weather. They either catch flu or a cold, which keeps them at bed. Despite the conscious wish to be healthy, this can happen due to a hidden yearning for attention from family and friends. Oftentimes, man wants to escape responsibilities. Hence he feels the deeper need to remain ill. This need for illness prevents healing.

Samir is constantly admonished by his family, friends and colleagues for his careless and forgetful nature. He keeps forgetting names of people and misplaces things quite frequently. He loses credibility due to his weakness. People do not entrust him work or responsibility due to his forgetfulness,.

When made to look within, he discovers the need to avoid responsibility. His childhood experiences of being ridiculed for not being able to accomplish trivial errands have led him to avoidance. Deep within, he feels relieved when he escapes responsibility to avoid being ridiculed. This wish to escape responsibility translates into a need for carelessness.

Being tormented by thoughts of past incidents, Samir finds it difficult to sleep. He sincerely wants to forget the past. This deeper wish to forget leads to forgetfulness. He forgets even essential things. However, Samir does not realize that he has invited forgetfulness only to escape from the past.

Samir needs to affirm to himself, *"It is good for me to remember everything that can help me in progressing towards my goal. It is safe for me to remember all the rich memories from my past."* When he releases the need to forget or be careless, he can actually welcome perfect health into his life.

If you discover any such hidden needs that are escape routes to shy away from responsibilities, you may want to repeatedly assert to your subconscious mind that owning responsibility is a divine quality and a stepping stone to progress. You may need to honestly and convincingly tell yourself that it is safe to take responsibility.

These were few examples that clarify how we nurture hidden needs that we do not consciously desire. There are many trivial needs that are hidden from our conscious awareness. We may not like to look at certain sights; we may not like to hear certain words; we may not like to smell certain odours.

Very often, we feel aversion for certain sights, sounds, words or odours, only because they trigger an associated painful memory within us. It is important to release such hidden needs and assert that it is now safe to experience the full breadth and depth of life.

Please keep the book aside and contemplate for a few minutes on the following points:

- Do you harbour any behavioural trait that often lets you down, despite all attempts to overcome it?
- Do you suffer from a frequent illness or an age-old disorder that doesn't heal?

- Look within to determine any hidden need to cling onto such traits or illness that offers apparent benefits.

If you have identified any hidden needs, then it is time to release it.

Releasing meditation

Many people find it difficult to let go of even trivial desires. This may lead to the accumulation of stress over time. When desires become overpowering, many people even need psychiatric counselling.

We will now consider a mediation known as the 'Releasing' meditation, which can help you to be rid of desires that do not actually serve your true progress. This meditation purifies your thinking and allows you to focus your attention on attaining mental and physical health.

There are many, who hesitate to express their feelings or thoughts. They can benefit immensely from this guided meditation and get rid of undesirable thoughts and tendencies from their subconscious mind. Let us look at the procedure for this guided meditation.

First set a timer for say, ten minutes. Close your eyes and sit in a comfortable posture.

Tell yourself, "*I am about to practice the Releasing meditation. I am going to reap the ultimate benefits from this meditation. I wish to get rid of unwanted thoughts, feelings and stress. Thanks for this opportunity to empty the unnecessary baggage that I have been hauling within me.*"

Remind yourself that even though you let go of all your desires during this meditation, it doesn't mean you will get nothing.

What is truly yours will definitely come to you, in abundance! What is not meant to be yours will disappear from your life. With this understanding, you need not hesitate to let go of things. Be assured that there is nothing to lose, and everything to be gained!

Ask yourself:

- What is it that I don't wish to see? What sights do I long to see?
- What is it that I don't want to hear? What words do I yearn to hear?
- Which tastes do I wish to avoid? Which tastes do I long for?
- Which odours do I dislike? Which fragrances do I like?
- What kind of touch do I repel? What kind of touch do I yearn?

After listening within to your answers to these questions, ask yourself, "*Is it possible for me to let go of all of these?*" Tell yourself, "*I can be free from all these things and lead a life of bliss. So it is safe to let go of all these desires. What is truly mine will come to me in abundance!*"

Tighten your fist and release it slowly while chanting "*Let go… Let go…*" Affirm to yourself that you have let go of your desires.

Think of the key activities in daily life that you either wish to do or avoid doing. We often have dreams of doing something big in life, of going someplace on vacation. Sometimes, we also wish to avoid certain obligations. Sometimes we fear facing difficulties or making mistakes while acting in the world. Bring all these to your awareness.

Ask yourself:

- Can I permit myself to make mistakes?
- Can I accept it if something does not work as I had planned?
- Can I lead a life of total freedom? Can I allow myself to be free?
- Can I let go of desires that bind me?

You will in most certainty get an affirmative answer from within. Again, tighten your fist and chant, "*Let go… Let go…*" while slowly releasing it. By now you will be in such a state that it no longer matters to you whether something happens in your life or not. You have let go of your fixations about how life should be or how it shouldn't be.

Check all hidden needs that you may have harboured. It is now time to uncover them. You need to know all those situations that you wish to escape. You wish to know the needs that you have nurtured to escape what you dislike.

Tell yourself, "*Can I allow myself to release these needs? They do not serve my true purpose; hence it is safe to let go of these needs. I release them fully, knowing that my true purpose will be served in letting go of them.*"

Tighten your fist and say, 'I am releasing all my hidden needs that do not serve me any more…" Release your fist slowly and chant, "*Let go… Let go… Let go…*"

Keep chanting "*Let go…*" for a while until you feel a deep sense of peace and release.

Before ending the meditation, proclaim your freedom and enjoy the beginning of a fresh life of freedom by raising your hands and chanting "*I am free... I am freedom!*"

Keep faith that by freeing yourself from desires you are not shooting yourself in the foot. You are purifying your mind. This will only help in unleashing your highest potential in life.

Finally, when the timer goes off, express your gratitude for the opportunity to free yourself and open your eyes.

You can modify this procedure as per your specific need. For example, instead of dealing with all types of desires at once, you can take one type at a time. One day you can work on desires of the tongue, the next day you can work on desires of the eyes, then ears, then the hidden needs and so on. This meditation is the key for you to embark on a journey to perfect health. Begin NOW!

◆ ◆ ◆

You can send your opinion or feedback on this book to :

Tejgyan Foundation, Pimpri Colony, P. O. Box 25,
Pimpri, Pune – 411017 (Maharashtra), INDIA
email : mail@tejgyan.com

Write for Us

We welcome writers, translators and editors to join our team. If you would like to volunteer, please email us at: englishbooks@tejgyan.org or call : +91 90110 10963 or +91 90110 13207

About Sirshree

Sirshree's spiritual quest which began during his childhood, led him on a journey through various schools of thought and meditation practices. His overpowering desire to attain the truth made him relinquish his teaching job. After a long period of contemplation, his spiritual quest culminated in the attainment of the ultimate truth. Sirshree says, **"All paths that lead to the truth begin differently, but end in the same way—with understanding. Understanding is the whole thing. Listening to this understanding is enough to attain the truth."**

Sirshree is the author of several spiritual books. His books have been translated in more than 10 languages and published by leading publishers such as Penguin and Hay House.

He is the founder of Tej Gyan Foundation, a not-for-profit organization committed to raising mass consciousness by spreading "Happy Thoughts" with branches in the United States, India, Europe and Asia-Pacific. Sirshree's retreats have transformed the lives of thousands and his teachings have inspired various social initiatives for raising global consciousness.

His works include more than 100 books and 3000 discourses. Various luminaries such as His Holiness the Dalai Lama, publishers Reid Tracy and Tami Simon and yoga master Dr. B. K. S Iyengar have released Sirshree's books and lauded his work. His book *The Warrior's Mirror*, published by Penguin, was featured in the Limca Book of Records for being released on the same day in 10 languages.

Tejgyan... The Road Ahead

What is Tejgyan?

Tejgyan is the existential wisdom of the ultimate truth, which is beyond duality. In today's world, there are people who feel disharmony and are desperately trying to achieve balance in an unpredictable life. Tejgyan helps them in harmonizing with their true nature, the Self, thereby restoring balance in all aspects of their life.

And then there are those who are successful but feel a sense of emptiness or void within. Tejgyan provides them fulfillment and helps them to embark on a journey towards self-realization. There are others who feel lost and are seeking the meaning of life. Tejgyan helps them to realize the true purpose of human life.

All this is possible with Tejgyan due to a very simple reason. The experience of the ultimate truth is always available. The direct experience of this truth is possible provided the right method is known. Tejgyan is that method, that understanding. At Tej Gyan Foundation, Sirshree imparts this understanding through a System for Wisdom – a series of retreats that guides participants step by step

Magic of Awakening Retreat

Magic of Awakening is the flagship self-realization retreat offered by Tej Gyan Foundation The retreat is conducted in two languages – Hindi and English. The teachings of the retreat are non-denominational (secular).

This residential retreat is held for 3-5 days at the foundation's MaNaN Ashram amidst the glory of mountains and the pristine nature. This ashram is located at the outskirts of the city of Pune in India, and is well connected by air, road and rail. The retreat is also held at other centres of Tej Gyan Foundation across the world.

Participate in the *Magic of Awakening* retreat to attain ageless wisdom through a unique simple 'System for Wisdom' so that you can:

1. Live from pure and still presence allowing the natural qualities of consciousness, viz. peace, love, joy, compassion, abundance and creativity to manifest.

2. Acquire simple tools to use in everyday life which help quieten the chattering mind, revealing your true nature.

3. Get practical techniques to access pure presence at will and connect to the source of all answers (the inner guru).

4. Discover missing links in practices of meditation *(dhyana)*, action *(karma)*, wisdom *(gyana)* and devotion *(bhakti)*.

5. Understand the nature of your body-mind mechanism to attain freedom from tendencies and patterns.

6. Learn practical methods to shift from mind-centred living to consciousness-centred living.

For retreats contact +919921008060 or email: mail@tejgyan.com

A Mini retreat is also conducted, especially for teens (14-17 years) during summer and winter vacations

MaNaN Ashram

Survey No. 43, Sanas Nagar, Nandoshi gaon, Kirkatwadi Phata, Sinhagad Road, Dist. Pune 411024, Maharashtra, India.

About Tej Gyan Foundation

Tej Gyan Foundation (TGF) was established with the mission of creating a highly evolved society through all-round self development of every individual that transforms all the facets of his/her life. It is a non-profit organization founded on the teachings of Sirshree. The foundation has received the ISO certification (ISO 9001:2015) for its system of imparting wisdom. It has centres all across India as well as in other countries. The motto of Tej Gyan Foundation is 'Happy Thoughts'.

TGF is creating a highly evolved society through:

- Tejgyan Programs (Retreats, Courses, Television and Radio Programs, Podcasts)

- Tejgyan Products (Books, Tapes, Audio/Video CDs)

- Tejgyan Projects (Value Education, Women Empowerment, Peace Initiatives)

TGF undertakes projects to elevate the level of consciousness among students, youth, women, senior citizens, teachers, doctors, leaders, organizations, police force, prisoners, etc.

Now you can register **online** for the following retreats

Maha Aasmani Niwasi Shivir
(5 Days Residential Retreat in Hindi)

Magic of Awakening Retreat
(3 Days Residential Retreat In English)

Mini Maha Aasmani Shivir
3 Days (Residential) Retreat for Teens

🔍 www.tejgyan.org

Books can be delivered at your doorstep by registered post or courier. You can request for the same through postal money order or pay by VPP. Please send the money order to either of the following two addresses:

WOW Publishings Pvt. Ltd.

1. Registered Office: E-4, Vaibhav Nagar, Near Tapovan Mandir, Pimpri, Pune 411017.

2. Post Box No. 36, Pimpri Colony Post Office, Pimpri, , Pune 411017

Phone No. : 9011013210 / 9623457873

You can also order your copy at the online store:

www.gethappythoughts.org

*Free Shipping plus 10% Discount on purchases above Rs. 300/-.

Also by Sirshree
Spiritual Masterpieces- Self Realisation books for serious seekers

1. **Answers that Awaken:** Access the Source of Wisdom within You
2. **Secret of the Third Side of the Coin :** Unraveling Missing Links in Spirituality
3. **You are Meditation :** Discover Peace and Bliss Within
4. **Essence of Devotion :** From Devotee to Divinity
5. **Dip into Oneness :** Beyond Knower, Known and Knowing
6. **The Unshaken Mind :** Discovering the Purpose, Power and Potential of your mind
7. **The Supreme Quest :** Your search for the Truth ends there where you are
8. **The Greatest Freedom :** Discover the key to an Awakened Living
9. **Seek Forgiveness & Be Free :** Liberation from Karmic Bondage

Self Help Treasures - Self Development books for success seekers

11. **The Source of Health:** The Key to Perfect Health Discovery
12. **Inner Ninety Hidden Infinity :** How to build your book of values
13. **Inner 90 for Youth :** The secret of reaching and staying at the peak of success
14. **The Source for Youth :** You have the power to change your life
15. **Inner Magic :** The Power of self-talk
16. **Self Encounter :** The Complete Path - Self Development to Self Realization
17. **The Five Supreme Secrets of Life :** Unveiling the Ways to Attain Wealth, Love and God
18. **You are Not Lazy :** A story of shifting from Laziness to Success
19. **Freedom From Fear, Worry, Anger :** How to be cool, calm and courageous

New Age Nuggets - Practical books on applied spirituality and self help

20. **The Source :** Power of Happy Thoughts
21. **Secret of Happiness :** Instant Happiness - Here and Now!
22. **Excuse me God... :** Fulfilling your wishes through the Power of Prayer and Seed of Faith
23. **Help God to Help You :** Whatever you do, do it with a smile
24. **Ultimate Purpose of Success :** Achieving Success in all five aspects of life
25. **Celebrating Relationships :** Bringing Love, Life, Laughter in Your Relations
26. **Everything is a Game of Beliefs :** Understanding is the Whole Thing

Profound Parables - Fiction books containing profound truths

27. **Beyond Life :** Conversations on Life After Death
28. **The One Above :** What if God was your neighbour?
29. **The Warrior's Mirror :** The Path To Peace
30. **Master of Siddhartha :** Revealing the Truth of Life and After-life
31. **Put Stress to Rest :** Utilizing Stress to Make Progress
32. **The Source @ Work :** A Story of Inspiration from Jeeodee

Other books related to *the* Source SERIES

 How to find Fulfilment at the Workplace

 Wings to the Source

 Living your values to Create an Ideal Life

 Heal from the Source

 A Roadmap for Beginners and a Myth Buster for Advanced Meditators

 Think Higher Rise Higher

 3 Laws, 3 Practices, 3 Principles to Build Beautiful Relationships

 7 Spiritual secrets to Overcome Setbacks

 Give and Get Happy Thoughts!

 A Pocket Guide to Love, Joy, Peace

For further details contact:

Tejgyan Global Foundation

Registered Office:
Happy Thoughts Building, Vikrant Complex, Near Tapovan Mandir, Pimpri, Pune 411017, Maharashtra, India.
Contact No: 020-27411240, 27412576
Email: mail@tejgyan.com

MaNaN Ashram:
Survey No. 43, Sanas Nagar, Nandoshi gaon, Kirkatwadi Phata, Sinhagad Road, Tal. Haveli, Dist. Pune 411024, Maharashtra, India.
Contact No: 992100 8060.

Hyderabad: 9885558100, **Bangalore:** 9880412588,

Delhi: 9891059875, **Nashik:** 9326967980, **Mumbai:** 9373440985

For accessing our unique 'System for Wisdom' from self-help to self-realization, please follow us on:

	Website	www.tejgyan.org
	Video Channel	www.youtube.com/tejgyan For Q&A videos: http://goo.gl/YA81DQ
	Social networking	www.facebook.com/tejgyan
	Social networking	www.twitter.com/sirshree
	Internet Radio	http://www.tejgyan.org internetradio.aspx

Online Shopping
www.gethappythoughts.org

Pray for World Peace along with thousands of others at 09:09 a.m. and p.m. every day